THE KEYS OF MY SOUL

ISBN: 9781020001109

45 Alternate Press, LLC
Hampton, VA

THE KEYS OF MY SOUL

RAN WALKER

For Zoë,
One day you will read this
and know how it all began.

THE FIRST MOVEMENT

OCTOBER 6, 2004

MILES THOMPSON

Richard and I had agreed to meet early this afternoon by the Alice in Wonderland sculpture in Central Park, just a few feet from a small pond where New Yorkers race their remote controlled boats. I glance at my watch and continue to observe couples walking hand-in-hand, young children chasing crumb-pecking pigeons, and weekend cyclists and in-line skaters with chiseled torsos moving rhythmically through the paths, animating this sprawling urban oasis.

I inhale the cool October air, losing myself in the mellow sounds of the music coming from my iPod. My boss, Diane Ford, the principal at Thelonius Monk Academy, had recommended the music during one of our most recent conversations about the direction, or lack thereof, of soul music. Admittedly, most of the music in my collection was recorded prior to 1984, and I don't know what to make of the newer artists currently in rotation on the local radio stations. It definitely isn't the same kind of music I used to compose for The Triumphs during the late seventies and early eighties.

I glance at my watch again. Richard is un-characteristically late.

A sweet fall breeze races across my face, and I look above the trees at the buildings framing the park from every angle. Central Park is an enormous garden courtyard surrounded by apartment buildings and skyscrapers. Lowering my eyes, I notice Richard coming into view, looking almost like he did over twenty years ago at Ellison-Wright College, but, as with most of my classmates, at least thirty extra pounds of buppie living have been added to his slight frame, and his hair is starting to noticeably gray.

I stand, removing my earbuds. "Richard!" I call out, waving my hands.

"My man Miles!" He laughs, gripping me in one of his trademark bear hugs. "How have you been?"

"Apparently not as good as you," I say, patting Richard's shoulder with one hand and poking playfully at his stomach with the other.

"You know how we do things down South. Look at *you* though. You look like you found the fountain of youth. You gotta tell me the secret."

"It's the music and this New York air. Good for the soul, you know?"

"I'll accept the music thing, but you can't tell me that the pollution up here is good for your health."

I shrug, attempting to keep a straight face but failing.

Richard angles his head, taking note of my shaved head. At first he eyes it with suspicion, then humor. "You killed the waves, man. I never thought I'd see the day."

I run my hand across my scalp. "You know how the ladies love bald-headed men," I joke.

Richard continues inspecting my head. "You know, it really doesn't look that bad. I mean, at least you don't have those brain-line grooves in your head like some guys."

"What are you trying to say?"

"Just paying you a compliment. But it's like my mama used to say, 'Some Negroes just can't take a compliment.'"

I double over laughing. When I can finally breath, I say, "Do you remember Allen Jacobson from school? He never should have cut his hair off."

Richard nods, lifting his hands as if creating a sculpture out of thin air. "That guy had an alien skull. His head was long like E.T.'s. And don't get me started on those grooves in his head. It looked liked someone had tried to rake that fool's brain."

"What ever happened to him?"

"Last I heard, he went back to Mississippi and became one of those trial lawyer millionaires back before the mass tort bubble popped. He married some beauty queen and had a few mini-E.T.s from what I hear."

"Good for him," I say. "Always happy to see one of our classmates come up."

"Me too. But dude still has some skull on him," Richard responds, laughing.

"Hungry?" I ask, although I already know my friend has never turned down a meal in all the years I have known him.

"Is George Clinton funky?"

"You're still flying out of LaGuardia at eight-thirty tonight, right?"

"Oh, yeah. My luggage is in the lobby at the hotel over near the airport."

"Well, I know a great place Uptown. The food's great, and it's quick. You'll have no problem making it to the airport on time, especially if you catch a gypsy cab."

"Sounds good," Richard says, popping the collar of

his black leather jacket in response to the cool breeze now whipping through the park.

Walking out of the park and onto the endless sidewalk that lines the avenue, I glance over at Richard. "It's good to see you," I finally say.

"Hey, man, what kind of friend would I be if I didn't holler at you while I was passing through your city?"

"I'm just saying it's good seeing a friendly face. That's all."

He nods his head understandingly.

I want to say more, but stop myself. I would never be able to tell him just how important his visit is. Actually, it's the first time I have felt completely alive in months.

THE AROMA OF CURRY, HOT SAUCE, AND FRIED chicken floats throughout Kathlyn's Corner, a small restaurant a few blocks off of 125th Street. It's as if the cooks want you to start curbing your appetite to their limited, but delicious, selections from the moment you enter.

I take in the scent, almost tasting the soulful/West Indian combinations dancing across my palate. I haven't been here in months, not since the nightmares ended. The restaurant still feels warm and inviting and reminds me of a time when Bettina would prepare home-cooked meals for the family. That seems like a lifetime ago, though. Now I am a different man—or at least I want to believe that. Sadly, this new man often eats microwaved meals from a stack of boxes in his freezer, unwilling to eat out alone and equally uninterested in making new friends. While Richard's presence is a nice change from the norm, the visit is heightened even more by the fact that I haven't been out socially in over three months.

Kathlyn's is packed, but we are still able to get a seat at a small table in the back.

"The food must be pretty good in here," Richard says, surveying the colorful surroundings. Several African-American art prints adorn the walls, and a huge African violet sits in the window, a nod to Kathlyn's sorority.

I signal the closest server, a beautiful mahogany-complexioned woman with striking dreadlocks, the two tones of her brown hair beautifully complementing each other.

"They don't have anything like this in Atlanta. Trust me," I tell Richard.

"The female or the food?"

"Both," I respond, smiling.

The server leans in to hand us two menus and takes our drink orders. Her name tag reads "Marjorie."

"Marjorie," I say, "we'd like two sweet teas."

"Sure. Two sweet iced teas coming up," she repeats, before she walks away. The way she moves is smooth enough to hold my breath in suspension for a moment.

"Sweet tea?" Richard says. "We're in New York City. Shouldn't the teas at least be Long Islands or something? You don't have to drive anywhere do you?"

I nudge Richard with my elbow. "I'm trying to put you on to one of the few spots in the city that even serves sweet tea."

"You can't be serious."

"It's definitely not like down South," I say, explaining how finding sweet tea in New York is like finding a cowboy in Brooklyn. For some reason, restaurants like to serve their tea unsweetened so you have to either dump artificial sweeteners into it or risk stirring in thirty packs of sugar that fall to the bottom of the glass like the imitation snowflakes in those small plastic souvenir balls filled with water.

"So tell me more about this new job," Richard says, peeling off his jacket. "Don't take this the wrong way, but you threw me for a loop when you came up here and started teaching."

He probably isn't the only one I confused when I packed up my things and left Atlanta. All I knew then was that I needed a major change in my life, and New York seemed far enough away from the life I had been living for the past twenty years to make a serious difference.

"I'm a music teacher over at the Thelonius Monk Academy for the Arts," I respond. "It's a new charter school in Harlem. About three hundred students. It's pretty nice. Right now I work with kids in junior high and teach them music appreciation and theory. I also give private lessons."

"I'm sure they're beside themselves having the legendary Miles Thompson on the faculty," Richard says.

"Very funny, man."

"No, I'm serious. I know there're a lot of people up here who know who you are. I mean, even Larry Blackmon and Maurice White probably still have panties thrown in their faces at the supermarket."

The people in the restaurant barely acknowledge our outburst of laughter. Just another thing I love about living in New York City.

"But tell me why here? I thought you would have returned to Mississippi or Tennessee or wherever the hell you're from if you were going to leave Atlanta," he continues.

Marjorie returns to our table with two large mason jars of sweet tea, a lemon wedge and mint leaf thrown in for flavor, but we have barely cracked open the menus and aren't ready to place our orders yet.

"I really don't know how I wound up here," I say. "Back then I was dazed and everything was a blur. The divorce. Dealing with Travis. I had to get away. And I just didn't want to go back home. I could've chosen to look at all of that stuff as a chance to crawl into a shell and die or as a chance to try something new. I feel like I ended up trying something new."

Talking to Richard puts me back into that familiar groove of discussing my problems with someone who can actually understand them. I didn't realize how much I had missed having a friend, a *real friend*, to talk to, face-to-face. Richard had been one of my groomsmen and had been there for me when I was going through the ordeal over Travis, and he had ultimately been there for me when things broke down between Bettina and me. If I couldn't talk real with Richard, then there was really no one in this world for me to talk real with.

"I understand," he responds. "How is Bettina doing these days anyway? I haven't seen her around town in a minute."

I take a sip of tea. It is so sweet that my lips immediately feel sticky, a good kind of sticky. It reminds me of sitting on the worn wooden porch of my grandmother's small house in Maben, Mississippi. "Last time I talked to Betina, she told me she had just gotten engaged but was taking everything slowly."

Richard shakes his head in disbelief. "So soon? Damn."

"Well, it's been about three years since the divorce."

"I didn't realize it had been that long." He takes a long swallow from his mason jar and smiles. "Oh, yeah. This is some good stuff here." He looks down into the sweet tea as if he can see the ingredients and determine their balance.

Pausing for a moment, he looks up at me. "How're you making it, man? I mean, we all miss Travis, too."

I can feel my throat tighten, and my eyes blink a few times before I open my mouth. "You know me, man. I'm just playing the hand I was dealt."

Richard swirls his tea around in the jar. "I've known you for more than twenty years, so you know I'm only asking you this question because you're my friend, right?"

I nod my head, a little nervous about what he is about to ask.

"You know you can't run away from the pain, don't you? I'm just hoping that your being here is really for the sake of 'trying something new' and not your trying to outrun the past."

Marjorie re-appears at our table, almost as if I willed her there. I already know I will deflect the question. I don't think I'm ready to talk about Travis to anyone just yet, including Richard.

Marjorie's dreadlocks are now pulled back into a ponytail. She is actually even more beautiful than I had previously thought. This time Richard and I go ahead and order the fried chicken specials. After all, he has a plane to catch in a few hours. As Marjorie turns to leave, she looks directly at me and smiles.

"I saw that," Richard says, lifting his glass in a mock toasting gesture. "See, people do know who you are!"

"No," I respond, stifling my laughter. "She just knows a single man flirting with her when she sees one."

SOMETIME AFTER THREE O'CLOCK IN THE morning, hours after Richard left for Atlanta, the nightmare returns. I sit up in my bed in a cold sweat, my one-bedroom apartment almost pitch black. The dream just seemed so real this time. Maybe that is because at one time it was.

I was there again, sitting at the dining room table, pecking on my laptop trying to figure out a tax software program Richard had talked me into buying. Bettina was in the kitchen whipping up her famous homemade lasagna. The smell was thick and delicious, and I couldn't wait to dig in. Travis was upstairs getting dressed for the football game over at his high school. I looked at the clock, and it read 6:10 p.m. In two hours, I would receive a call that my only son had been murdered, but my dreams haven't evolved that far yet. Lately it seems like they are variations on a theme, as if my mind is trying to go back in time and slow things down to replay everything that happened, tempting me to change what cannot be changed. Like why didn't Travis stay for lasagna? Why was he in such a hurry to get to that football game anyway? Did the kid who killed him ever consider the possibility that he would murder my son when he placed that nine-millimeter into the waistband of his pants? The detectives told me that my son had just been in the wrong place at the wrong time. That's not the kind of thing a parent wants to hear. At the time, I wanted to throw something into a wall when I thought about how a second here or there could have kept my son alive.

My dreams don't do anything but wake me up with a feeling of helplessness, teasing me since I can't go back and change anything. Living in this apartment alone doesn't do much in the way of comfort either. I just wake up and pace the floor. Then I put on Miles Davis's *Kind of Blue* album to calm me down. But sometimes it gets so bad I have to just drop to my knees and keep praying until I fall asleep on the floor next to my bed.

I have several pictures of Travis here in the apartment, but only his junior class picture is framed on my dresser. It's the last school picture that he took and the way that I choose to remember his face. I keep the other ones in a small box on the top shelf of my bedroom closet. I can only take having one picture of my son on display in my apartment. It would be too painful to see his face all over this place.

As a parent who has lost a child, there is one thing I know to be true: you never stop hurting. It just hurts in different degrees, depending on the day. Some days it feels like I am walking a mile in shoes filled with broken glass and alcohol; other days it feels like every part of me is normal, but there is still something basic, something fundamental, missing. That's the piece, I suspect, that will never be filled. Each day is an emotional lottery where you understand that there are various levels of losing.

After the divorce I figured New York would heal that pain and frustration and help me move forward with my life. For a while things got better, much better, but then the nightmares started. That last night of my son's life played out every other night in my head for months. The dreams gradually faded into dreams that I couldn't remember. I might have still been having them, but I didn't know it because I would wake up unable to remember them. I wanted to believe they had simply left, but tonight whatever thoughts I had assumed were dormant were somehow re-awakened. Maybe I should have talked about Travis to Richard today, but instead I held back, only to wake up in the middle of the night with it stuck in my head like an eerie, almost forgotten melody.

2

OCTOBER 6, 2004

JA KENDRICK BROWN

By the time I get off the C train at 125th, I already see my boys standing on the platform. Yusef and Quentin look like they just got here a few minutes before me. Yusef is carrying around the bongo drums we copped off this Nigerian vendor a few months back when we decided to really step up our shit. Quent likes to say he's always carrying his instrument around on him. I guess it must be like that for singers. And that nigga can blow, too! He's what them folks in the Dirty South call a "sanger." He can sing a big girl up out a thong! As for me, I got Angela up under my arm in the new carrying bag I got with some of the funds over the last month. Angela is my keyboard. And I got mad skillz, if I must say so myself.

Me and my boys been hustling the trains for roughly a year now, switching lines by the week and adjusting our gig to the cash flow. Sometimes the 2 or 3 will be hot or the 4 or 5 will be on. This week we're working the A, C, E lines. What we'll probably do is hop on the A first, since it's an express and it's easier to hit up folks when the train ain't making stops every minute.

"Yo, Yusef," I say, dapping him with my free hand.

"A'ight, son," Yusef says, leaning in with his shoulder.

Quent reaches out to dap me. "Ja, it's 'bout you, baby!"

"You know me," I say, gripping him and leaning in with my shoulder. "I gots to be Nigga-rachi wit mines."

I had picked up that nickname from my boys from way back in the day the first time they heard me on the keys. And I know I've been known to act a fool when I play, but I can't help it. I feel like I was born with my fingers on the keys. One of my partners from back in the day, Peter Stein, used to call me a black Liberace because of the way I played. I was like "whatever." One night, though, I was watching TV and I saw this clown-ass dude on TV banging the hell out of a monster-size piano, hands dipped in that iced-out shit. He looked like a pimped out muppet, but those skillz was on point like a motherfucker. When I found out that dude was Liberace, I was like, "Yo, that ain't cool at all." That's when Quent started fucking with me by calling me Nigga-rachi. After a while, I just got used to the name and embraced it. Although that Liberace dude was way out there, he was the nicest cat I ever saw on the keys. And working it out with that iced out shit, too! I could've probably lived off that pinky ring for ten years.

"A'ight. What y'all wanna do today?" I ask. We always agree on what our play list is gonna be. "I'm feeling like knocking out some Stevie Wonder today."

Yusef smiles. "Always old school with you, huh?"

They already know the answer to that question. I'm definitely a true hip-hop head, but back in the day the music had more melody, so I like it when I get a chance to light into something that people can immediately get with. That gives me a chance to really groove. It's boring as hell playing some of these new tracks where the song ain't nothing but a beat with no melody. Plus, my boys don't know that I keep my skillz on the keys sharp by rocking that classical shit when I'm not around them. I'm into Beethoven and Greig, but when I really want to work out the fingers, I get into some of that Franz Liszt shit. Oh snap! That dude is so off the fucking chains! That's how I wanna be.

"You feeling Stevie?" I ask, turning to face Quent.

He steps back from Yusef and me and starts singing the first lines of "All I Do." His voice blasts out all over the subway station. Not missing a beat, I take Angela out the bag, batteries fully powered, and pick up the chords and bass line on the keys. Yusef leans back against the beam behind him and places the bongos between his legs, letting loose. And there we are: jamming the hell out of Stevie's "All I Do" on the platform. I pull the beanie off my dreadlocks and place it on the ground in front of us. After all, if you're gonna jam like this, you gotta give people a chance to tip you.

WE USUALLY HOOK UP AFTER SCHOOL LETS OUT and make out well before winding down after rush hour. We sometimes hustle a Benjamin or so and split it by three. I'm no fool though. I know part of the appeal to what we do is that we're so young. I'm fifteen, Yusef is fifteen, and Quent is the baby at fourteen. I know these people would rather see us jamming music on the subway than sticking them up when they get off at their stops. Plus, I just ain't into doing the stick-up thing. I'm just into my music.

We usually shut down for the day just after 7:30, right before it starts getting dark. By that time, things start slowing down, unless it's a Friday night. And the beautiful thing about each line is that they all run through heavy corporate spots. A corporate sista will step onto the train at 59th Street, and there we are, sitting in her car, jamming her favorite songs, massaging her mental, saying, "Baby, don't let that job stress you. Relax. We got you." Or a dude will jump on from Wall Street, and we hit him with that song that reminds him of that girl from back in the day that he used to holla at—before the stocks and bonds and shit. See, what makes us different than the other people hustling on the trains is that we really have a purpose with our music.

Most of the time we just wrap up because we're hungry, not because the clock says this or that. Quent is kind of husky, and he's not one to skip too many meals, so I guess you could say we just time our day with his hunger pangs. Yusef says that Quent reminds him of Peabo Bryson. Singing, maybe. But Quent is a yellow nigga with freckles and a red Afro, and the last time I checked, Peabo was on some smooth, debonair shit. They don't look nothing alike, but they sound pretty close, and Quent might have Peabo beat when it comes to tearing up some fried chicken.

We head back up to 125th and grab some Popeye's. After we finish up, I'm gonna hop on the train and see if I can find some real keys to bang on for minute. Don't get it twisted, I love my Angela, but there's nothing like having those real ivories beneath my fingers.

I BEEN WALKING AROUND SCOPING FOR A MUSIC instrument shop still open, but it just ain't going down tonight. I'm getting tired too, and I know I need to camp out somewhere for a while or just hop the C train headed back Uptown.

I just hope that Daryl's not there. I can't stand that nigga! I keep hoping someone'll pop that fool, but till this day, he's still here, raising hell. I take some change out of my pocket and step to a payphone on the corner. I dial the number to the crib, hoping my big sis will answer, but she don't. I decide to press my luck and go on home anyway. If that bitch-nigga Daryl is there, I'll just bail the hell on out and crash on the C train tonight and go back in the morning.

I got Angela standing up in her case, resting against my leg. I can feel a few of my dreads hanging loose when I rest my chin on the case. I close my eyes. I just wanna get some sleep, kick back and cop some Z's. Angela almost falls on the floor when the train stops, and I wake up just in time to not miss my stop.

Coming out of the station, I have to walk two blocks over and one block up to get to my apartment building. I'm scanning the streets, checking for Daryl's forest green Hummer. I don't see it parked anywhere. Cool.

I take out my key and go inside. The elevator is broke this week (and every other week), so I take the stairs up three floors, walk down to the end of the hall, and unlock the door to the apartment. The TV is on, so Sherita must be here.

"Sherita," I call out, propping Angela up against the wall in the kitchen. "Sherita, you up in here?"

I don't hear a response so I walk around to the bedroom. This is a one-bedroom apartment, and when I do manage to stay here, I sleep on the couch in the main room. I open the door and see that the lights are turned out. I turn them on and see my older sister stretched out across the bed, buck-ass naked, face down, like she just passed out.

"Sherita," I say, walking over to her. I'm hoping the light'll be bright enough to wake her up.

I walk around the edge of the bed and touch her shoulder. It's warm and damp. She moves and starts groaning something. Ol' girl looks straight-up pitiful. And it's times like this when I really want to kill that nigga Darryl. My sister is high out her mind, and her man is out there somewhere slinging that shit, fucking up someone else's family.

Most of the time we don't run the heat up in this piece 'cause that Con Ed bill is a motherfucker, but I don't want her to freeze lying out here on top of the covers either. I try to pull back the sheets on her bed, but she's laid out like a marble slab. Even though she's not all that big, if you try to pull her when she's sleep, it's like tussling with a sumo wrestler, so I have to get her to wake up enough so she can help me move her.

"Sherita, wake up for a second. You need to get under the covers."

She grunts at me and swats her arm in my direction. Back in the day, my sister used to play b-ball at her school, and she's still pretty strong. I have to step out of her way before I fuck around and get knocked out.

"I'm *so* tired," she says, dropping her arm back over the edge of the bed.

"I know," I say. "It'll only take a second though."

I pull at the sheets while pushing her, kind of rocking her out of the way. Eventually she starts to wake up, and she edges over the top of the sheets and turns to get under them. I look away.

"You already seen my ass, baby brother. You scared to see my titties?" she says.

I can barely make out what she's saying, and it don't really matter if I can hear her or not because she's high as a satellite, and she don't really know what she's doing when she gets like this.

She closes her eyes, and I walk back over by the

door and turn off the lights. I go over to the couch in the main room and kick off my Timberlands. I take off my beanie and let my dreads fall on my shoulders. The room ain't that big, but the dark makes it look like it's just stretching on forever, like deep space.

I think about Liszt and remember that someone told me he was like that dude Liberace back in the day. Then I think about composing my own pieces and performing them on stage at Carnegie Hall.

Before I close my eyes, though, I think about me and my sister and our daily struggle, and I pray like hell that one day I can get us both up out of here, leave all this madness behind, and never look back.

3

OCTOBER 11, 2004

MILES THOMPSON

The Thelonius Monk Academy, or TMA, as the faculty and students refer to it, is located on the first and second floors of an older building on the west side of 120th Street, just off of 8th Avenue. The school is supposed to function as a "liberal arts junior high magnet school for urban students seeking to enter into a performance arts school for their secondary education." Or so says the flashy four-color brochures we send out. As Richard once referred to it, I teach the kids who want to go to the *Fame* schools, like LaGuardia.

I'm one of the newest faculty members, and because of the size of the building, I don't even have an office. I've been told those kinds of things come with seniority. It doesn't bother me though. For the last month or so I've just been coming in to work early and using my classroom as an office. I normally wake up around four in the morning from the nightmares, and then hop in the shower, get dressed, and head to the train station. Sometimes I walk the twenty or so blocks to the school, if the weather's not bad.

Today the weather is clear, but the temperature is dropping pretty quickly these days. I reach in my closet and pull out a red turtleneck sweater, my black leather jacket, and a black toboggan. The sun is just starting to rise. Back in Atlanta, birds would be chirping about this time, signaling a new day, but here, the only thing you can hear are the mild roars of vehicles passing through the streets.

The blocks flow by effortlessly, but I know I'll have to resort to catching the subway soon because I could easily get slammed in the face by some pretty frigid hawk in the coming weeks, given the direction I have to walk. Even at the early hour of 5:00 a.m., there is still more movement going on than you would expect to see at this time of day.

When I reach the building, I fish around in my pocket for the front door key. Just as I go to open the door, a voice calls out from behind me.

"Miles, hold the door!" Teresa Baptiste walks briskly toward me holding a box in front of her, her purse sliding down into the angle of her arm.

"Good morning. You need some help?" I ask, extending my hands toward her package, while balancing the door against my leg.

"Well, sure—if you don't mind."

She hands me the box and steps around me into the building. "How was your weekend?"

"Nice. Uneventful—you know, the way I like it."

I follow her, walking down the dimly lit halls. She steps over to the wall and turns on the light switch, allowing us to navigate ourselves more securely to her classroom.

"You can set that box over there on the table against the window," she says and adds, "I really appreciate it." She smiles at me, a very radiant and beautiful smile.

Teresa is about 5'6" with a reddish brown complexion. Her hair is a complementary dark brown, shoulder length press. And because she wears a stylish, yet simple, pair of eyeglasses, she gives the appearance of someone who is too young to teach here. She is wearing a camel colored three quarter inch trench coat that is opened to reveal a cream cashmere sweater. Although the outfit is conservatively business casual, it's not hard to see that she is very much into fitness. She's married to a Haitian playwright who has had a few productions running Off-off Broadway, and they have two boys, both kids a few years too young for admission to TMA. She's easily the most attractive woman at this school, as well as one of the most highly regarded teachers.

"I thought I was the only one who bothered to come in this early," I say, admiring how she has set up her room. She teaches history, and there are pictures of different African-American leaders and artists on the various walls. Next to a picture of John Coltrane is a picture of Thelonius Monk, the school's namesake.

"Sometimes I like to get a head-start, too," she says, smiling. "Wanna get some coffee?"

"Sure," I respond, although I don't really drink coffee.

We walk down the hall to the teacher's lounge and she starts up a pot. We sit on two perpendicularly situated couches as we wait for the coffee to brew. I feel very comfortable around her, but that probably has more to do with her being from Jackson, Tennessee, which almost makes her a homegirl.

"Anything exciting going on in your class?" she asks. Her face is animated in such a way that you would think that it was not that early in the morning after all.

"I'm going to be lecturing on bee-bop this week, and I'm hoping to draw some connections between that and hip-hop," I say.

"Sounds fun."

"I believe that it will be."

Sometimes I can't believe I get paid to share what I love with young minds. Being Uptown with all of these diverse cultures, my students have already been largely exposed to a myriad of music, so the classroom discussions tend to take on lives of their own. I only had to give out one "C" last quarter, so I feel like I'm really connecting with my students.

Teresa stands and walks over to the cupboard, taking out two mugs and filling them. "How do you like your coffee?" she asks.

I look at her sheepishly. "I don't really drink a lot of coffee, so I don't have much of a frame of reference for how to flavor it."

"You don't drink coffee?" she asks in mock disbelief. "I don't know what I would do without a cup or two to get my day started."

She takes some sugar and places it in each mug. Reaching to open the small refrigerator in the lounge, she takes out a small carton of cream and adds equal amounts to each coffee. "Here," she says, handing me one of them. "Try this, and let me know if you like it."

I take the mug and hold it against my lips, inhaling the aroma. It is sweet and inviting, but I know the only reason I am even holding this is because Teresa made it for me. I place the mug to my lips, and the heat warms my face. I sip slowly, allowing the strong, bitter flavor to spread across my palate. The dissolved sugar crystals are almost non-existent until they catch on my taste buds at the last possible second. Tasting it is like a joke on myself when I realize that I've avoided drinking coffee all of these years because my mother had once told me that drinking it would stunt my growth. Now at 6'2" I am still wary of coffee. The flavor isn't bad, but it's definitely an acquired taste, like beer. I nod in approval at Teresa, taking another sip.

"Well, I know that this store brand coffee the school buys is not the greatest, but on a cool morning like this, it'll do." She takes another sip of her coffee and leans against the counter.

I set the mug on the small table in front of me. Massaging my hands, I pop my fingers. I know it's a bad habit, but I've always found that it relaxes me. Gradually it dawns on me that we're alone in this room, and I begin to feel slightly uncomfortable. I would hate for something to get back to her husband, a misunderstanding from someone walking in on us this early in the morning.

I am preparing to excuse myself and go to my room when she asks, "So what was it like performing with The Triumphs?"

Up until this very moment, nothing much had ever been said of my former career. I imagine that most of the faculty members probably knew I was the lead songwriter and keyboardist for The Triumphs back in the late seventies and early eighties. As a band, we had met with a little bit of success, culminating with an album certified "gold" by the Recording Industry Association of America in 1984. I don't know why I am so surprised by the question though. After all, I *am* teaching a music class.

I look over at Teresa, and her face is expectant, her dimples framing her smile. I respond, "You know, I can honestly say that it was great while it lasted."

"Do you think that you guys will ever get back together and tour again?"

If I had a dime for every time I got asked that question, I'd be wealthier than Warren Buffett, but I can't bring myself to explain the details of why the band split up in the first place. "We'll see," I say. "Right now I just want to focus on being the best teacher I can be."

"That's sweet. A little idealistic, but very sweet," she says, putting her mug down.

"Maybe, but I need to know that I'm making a difference right now. Here, I feel like I am."

She walks over and picks up the mug that I haven't touched in the last few minutes and takes it over to the sink, rinsing it out. She turns to face me. "You *are* making a difference. The children really enjoy your class. I can see it in their faces."

"Really?"

"You ain't know, Mr. Thompson?" she responds, imitating our students. She pats me on my chest as she walks out of the faculty lounge back down the hall to her classroom.

MY CLASSROOM IS AT THE END OF THE HALL ON the first floor, near a door that leads out into the courtyard where the students have recess. The room is a little bit larger than Teresa's, but I don't get much of an opportunity to use the additional space because of the baby grand piano resting majestically to the side of my desk, just a few feet away from the window. The blinds beside the piano are drawn shut so as to not let the sunlight beat up on the color of the wood. I haven't really used the piano much for my music appreciation classes, but it's the heart and soul of the lessons I provide after school. Right now I teach about ten children a week, two lessons a day after school. The money is a nice supplement to my salary, but I just enjoy working with the students. And to be truthful, I didn't exactly come to New York broke.

In addition to the money I was already getting

quarterly from ASCAP for the songs I wrote for The Triumphs and a few other recording artists, I came into a windfall about four years ago when two different rappers sampled from my publishing catalog. One of the rappers, D-Sweetness, a sultry young woman who was marketed almost entirely on her bare-clad appearance, was a bust—no pun intended. Her album didn't get much support from the label. It was pretty much like a poot in the wind, and the label only released one single —and it wasn't the song with my sample. But I did get mechanical royalties. The other rapper, Big Boze, sampled one of my songs, and it wound up becoming the hip-hop anthem of the summer a few years back. The only thing I regret about the song is that it didn't really begin to pick up rotation until after Travis died. He was into hip-hop, so he might have actually liked the song.

My son was more the athlete. Basketball was his game. At 6'2", my own height, he played shooting guard. He had just made the starting line-up the previous season and was looking forward to helping his team go to the state championship that season. It seemed like Travis had been born with a basketball in his hands. In many ways, I was hoping he would have gravitated more towards music than sports. Growing up, I played basketball in school, but by the time I got to college, I was pretty deep into music. I played intramural basketball when Travis was little, so that's probably how his fascination got piqued. When he got to junior high, I wasn't surprised when he went out for basketball, but on some level, deep down, I was kind of disappointed when he didn't tryout for band. I was hoping that music would have taken root in his soul like it had in mine. Maybe I didn't do enough to steer him that way, but it was what it was, and I was proud of him all the same.

I look up at the wall and notice that it's a few minutes before my students will start trickling in. Maybe what I say today will touch somebody, and on some level I will be forgiven for whatever mistakes I made with my own son.

4

————

9 YEARS EARLIER

JA KENDRICK BROWN

I was six, just a little shorty, when they took Mama away. I remember that day like it was yesterday. I was with Mama and Sherita in the same apartment I live in now. It was just a regular Saturday in June, and me and Sherita had been watching something on TV in the main room. It was almost noon, and Mama was still in her room with the door closed.

"Mama must be real tired," I said to Sherita.

Sherita stood up from the couch. "I'ma go and check on her. See if she's a'ight."

Sherita walked down the short hall to the bedroom and tried to open the door. "Mama! It's me! Open up!"

"Who are you?" Mama yelled. It didn't even sound like Mama. Mama usually had a nice, sweet voice. This voice was heavy and stressed out, like Mama was scared or amped up on something.

"Mama, you a'ight in there?" Sherita asked.

I hopped off the couch and walked over to Sherita.

I could hear rustling and knocking sounds going on inside the room. Finally, Mama's voice came through the door. "I want you and your brother to listen to me," she said. "Something is really wrong right now, and I'm very scared."

"Mama, what's wrong? Let me in," Sherita said, twisting the doorknob. It didn't budge.

"I can't," Mama said. "I don't trust you right now, baby. I need you to work with me and help me trust you."

Tears ran down my cheeks like I was holding my face up to the rain. What was Mama talking about? Was someone in there with her? Why was she talking crazy like that? I looked up at Sherita, and she put her arm around me and pulled me closer. My tears wet up the side of her t-shirt.

All of a sudden there was a loud bang on the door, and we jumped. I looked up at Sherita, and she looked just as scared as me.

"Sherita! Kendrick!" Mama screamed through the door. She banged on the door like she was using both fists. "Sherita! Kendrick! You out there?"

"Yes, Mama," Sherita said. She leaned in closer to the door. "We're right here."

"Where is Kendrick?"

"He's right here, Mama," Sherita said.

"Baby, I don't trust you right now. Let me hear Kendrick's voice. Let me hear his voice!" She banged against the door again, and my heart jumped in my chest.

"I'm here, Mama! I'm here!" I yelled so she could hear me over the pounding.

"I just needed to know where both y'all are," she said. "Don't be scared. I'm just having some problems right now, and I need you two to pray with me. OK?"

"Yes, Mama," Sherita said.

"Now, Kendrick," Mama said, "I want you to go get the Bible off the bookshelf in there."

I ran over to the small bookshelf near the front door. Besides an old worn-out set of *Childcraft* Encyclopedias, there wasn't much else there. I found the

Bible lying on top, grabbed it, and ran back over to the door. "I got it!"

"Good, Kendrick. Good. You know, you was always a good boy," she said. "I need to know that you and me are on the same page though."

I looked at Sherita. She had this glazed look that scared the hell out of me. Then I got this aching knot in the pit of my stomach, like something real bad was about to happen.

Mama kept on. "See my finger under this door? Touch my finger with yours! I need to know that you're with me on this!"

I whispered to Sherita, "What's wrong with Mama?"—but Mama overheard us.

"Are you two out there whispering? You're both trying to do me in!" she yelled.

Sherita grabbed the doorknob and began rocking it back and forth. "Mama, let me in so I can help you."

There was a sound like an explosion going off as Mama pounded both fists against the door in one big boom. "Stay away from me!"

Sherita pulled me back from the door, and we went back into the main room. She sat me on the couch and started pacing the floor. I could hear Mama screaming through the door, "You don't love me! Nobody loves me!"

"What are we gonna do?" my sister asked. I don't think she expected me to answer, but I did anyway.

"Call Auntie Sarah," I said.

Sherita stopped for a moment, like she was really thinking about it, and then the beating on the door got worse. I was scared Mama would bust through the door and kill us.

"Kendrick!" Mama called out. "Come over here and pray with me. I don't trust your sister. She's got too much whore in her!"

"I'm scared," I told Sherita. She took my hand and held it.

"Kendrick! Kendrick! Don't do this to me! Pray with me! Pray with your mother!" Mama's voice was getting crazier and crazier.

Sherita leaned down and told me to go to the door and pray with Mama while she called Auntie Sarah.

I sat on the floor by the door with the Bible clutched to my chest with one hand and the other hand touching Mama's finger under the door. Mama prayed like she was possessed for a few minutes and then started cussing up a storm—but she was still praying. It seemed like I sat on the floor by that door all day.

By the time Auntie Sarah had gotten to us from her crib in Brooklyn, I was pretty fucked up. My lips almost stuck together from all the snot running out my nose. I just couldn't stop crying, and I didn't have no extra hand to wipe my face.

After Auntie Sarah came, the only thing I remember was her calling for an ambulance.

I WAS SIX YEARS OLD WHEN I SAW MAMA GETTING poked with needles and carried out, strapped to a stretcher. Sherita told me later on that what we saw that day was called a "manic episode." She said that Mama was bipolar. I didn't know what the hell that was, but she told me it meant that Mama had this condition where she could get real worked up or real depressed and needed to take medicine to control it.

Auntie Sarah stayed with Sherita and me for about a month after that, and Mama ended up in a mental institution for a year. When I asked Sherita why Mama was gone for so long she told me that Mama wasn't taking her medicine, so they wouldn't release her. They said that without the medicine, Mama could hurt someone or even herself.

Mama eventually got well enough to come home though, but she was pretty drugged up at first. Before long, she got down to about two medications a day, and everything went back to normal, the way it was before she got sick. That's when she gave me the keyboard—during that downtime.

Although I don't really remember exactly why Mama gave me the keyboard, Sherita says that when I was little, I used to bang on pots and pans in the kitchen, that whenever music would come on, I would always start dancing. I guess Mama figured that a keyboard was less noise than some drums, or maybe it was just that Mama always liked the piano.

The keyboard was pretty big, and I was just a little shorty when she gave it to me. She also gave me this book with big pages on how to play it. I guess she forgot that I was only seven and could barely read a book, let alone teach myself music.

One day while I was messing around on my keyboard, Mama came in and watched me. I didn't see her at first. I can't even remember what I was playing, but I hadn't been at it that long. After a while, I got the feeling that someone was watching me, so I stopped and turned around.

"Ooh, Mama! You scared me! Sneaking up on me like that," I said.

I looked up at her face and saw Mama was crying.

"What's wrong, Mama? Why you crying?" I said, becoming scared.

I was so caught up in her tears that I didn't notice her smiling. For a minute we just stared at each other.

Finally, Mama said, "Kendrick, that was beautiful."

I wish I could remember what I was playing that

made her cry. I was still getting familiar with the scales, so my ability to read music was pretty limited—and my ability to play it wasn't much better.

What Mama would tell me next, I will always hold in my heart: Music will open many doors for you.

I still believe that.

MAMA HAD BEEN HOME FOR TWO YEARS SINCE that first manic episode, and we had finally gotten back to being a happy family again. And then one morning she just refused to get out of bed. By the time I came home from school, I found her lying in the bed like she was sleeping. The rest is a blur.

The final word was that Mama had gotten depressed and swallowed too many sleeping pills. As far as Sherita and I knew, Mama ain't never been depressed. Dr. Neal Blake told me after the funeral that sometimes people who are bipolar only have to get depressed one time for them to go over the edge. I wanna believe Mama just took too many pills by accident. I really wanna. But on some level, I know better.

When I was nine years old I lost the most important person in my world, my mother, Angela Yvette Brown, and to this day, I still don't understand why.

5

____

OCTOBER 21, 2004

MILES THOMPSON

The gypsy cab lets me off at Astor Place, and I walk down to the Public Theater. The congestion down here in the East Village is different from Harlem. There are a lot of students, artists, and slumming trust fund babies wandering about, looking for excitement.

It's a cool Thursday evening around 7:30, and my wool pea coat is buttoned tightly, my scarf wrapped high so that it catches my earlobes. I scan the crowd standing in front of the theater, praying my date can recognize me. I told her that my coat would be charcoal grey and that I'd be wearing a pair of navy blue slacks. She said she would be wearing a white trench coat. I should have called off the blind date then. If she was wearing a white trench coat in late October, she probably had a little poodle named Her Majesty. Definitely not my type.

Frank Lassiter, one of my workout partners at the neighborhood gym, told me he had someone he wanted me to meet. Her name was Melody, he said. She was a forty-year-old divorcee who had become a recent transplant to the City from none other than Secaucus, New Jersey, right on the other side of the Lin-

33

coln Tunnel. Apparently she was a good friend of Gina, Frank's wife, and Frank recommended me as the guy who should show Melody around. I hardly missed the joke since I hadn't even been in New York City for two years, but Melody had spent at least ten years living less than fifteen miles away.

A few lazy conversations later, accompanied by the loneliness that comes with the holiday season, I found myself asking her out to go see a Kenny Leon play over in the East Village. This, of course, was before the white coat comment.

Scanning the crowd I suddenly find myself staring at a very striking golden complexioned woman wearing a crème colored trench coat. Her hair is a glimmering shoulder length, and she's smiling at me.

"Excuse me, but you must be Miles Thompson," she says, approaching me and extending her hand.

I smile. "And you must be Melody Lithcott."

"It's good to finally meet you."

At roughly 5'4", she looks remarkably younger than the age Frank shared with me earlier. In fact, she's extremely attractive. Part of me wants to plan the evening out, mapping a way into her bedroom. The other part wants to treat the situation casually, since I just met her, and take it slowly to see where it goes. Back in the day with the Triumphs, when women were throwing themselves at us and sneaking through security to get to our hotel rooms, I would have done her without question. After all, what was there to think about? Why make a physical situation any deeper than it has to be? But that was before Bettina and Travis.

After I hand the ticket taker our tickets, we walk to our seats, and I help her out of her coat. She is wearing a form-fitting long sleeve shirt with a scoop neck that reveals the top of her very shapely breasts. Her waist is slender, and her hips appear to be robust and sexy in her snug denim jeans. Almost like clockwork, the other men in the general vicinity exercise careful use of their peripheral visions to admire Melody's body, so as to not offend their own dates. It's not hard to see that she works out and takes care of her body. The thought of seducing her returns to my head immediately, but I shrug it off. At this point in my life, I'm still trying to figure out what I really want, and I'm careful about needlessly complicating things.

We both settle into our seats as the lights flash, indicating that it's time for the show to start. When the curtains open, I feel her leg rub lightly against mine.

———

JUST AS THE INTERMISSION STARTS AND THE HOUSE lights come up, Melody stretches slightly. We step out into the lobby, and she excuses herself to go to the restroom.

People from all walks of life crowd the room. Occasionally I'll see someone glance in my direction, as if they recognize me, but for the most part, people are just doing their own thing, paying me no mind.

It's refreshing going out to a nice event like this, especially since I have dated very little since I got here. I imagine Melody standing there, removing her coat, and I smile. I'm starting to reconsider on closing that deal. Tonight? Don't know. I could use the companionship in light of all I've been dealing with over the last few weeks though.

As I ponder the fate of my evening, I hear a soft, recognizable voice calling out from behind me.

"Miles!" the voice squeals, as I turn to see Teresa Baptiste.

It takes me a moment to notice her husband standing next to her, holding her hand.

"Teresa," I say, smiling. "How are you?"

"Great." Turning to her husband, she says, "Honey, this is Miles Thompson. He works with me at TMA. He teaches music."

"Jean-Claude Baptiste," her husband says, introducing himself. He gives me a firm handshake. "I thought I recognized you. I'm a big fan of your music."

Jean-Claude is taller than me by a few inches. I venture to say that he is about 6'5", a tower over Teresa. His manicured dreadlocks are pulled back into a ponytail, and he is wearing a v-neck cashmere sweater under his sports coat.

"Thank you," I respond. I want to offer a similar compliment about his plays, but I have never seen any of them. Instead I shift focus. "So what do you think of the play so far, your being well-steeped in playwriting and all?"

His face lights up. "The pacing is pretty good. Kenny has done an excellent job. I can't wait to see how the next half will go."

As the three of us speak casually about the play, I find myself occasionally glancing over at Teresa. She appears to be enjoying our collective dialogue. While facing Jean-Claude, I can see Teresa with my peripheral vision, and I swear she looks like she's checking me out.

I continue talking to both of them, trying to ignore this look Teresa is giving me, when I feel someone brush against my shoulder. It's Melody.

I quickly introduce Melody to the Baptistes as my friend.

"Well, we should probably be getting back to our seats," Jean-Claude says. "I think they're about to start dimming the lights."

I extend my hand to him again. "It was good

meeting you." And as an after comment: "And seeing you again, Teresa."

Teresa looks at me distantly and smiles. "Good seeing you. And good to meet you too, Melody."

Melody and I follow them back into the theater as the lights flash. We sink into our seats and the curtains open, but this time my mind is a long way from what is on the stage.

"I CAN'T TELL YOU HOW MANY TIMES I'VE GOTTEN lost since I started riding the trains," Melody says, placing her margarita on the coaster in front of her.

After the play ended, we walked over to University Avenue and ordered drinks at a small, quaint Mexican restaurant known for it's fabulous bartenders and even more fabulous prices.

"I can understand that," I say, chuckling. "Someone had to sit me down with a Metro map and break down how the City is divided into halves, east and west. After that, it's just a matter of knowing exactly where certain neighborhoods lie along the grid."

"Don't you sound smart?" Melody offers playfully.

"Well, I must have slept at a Holiday Inn Express last night," I respond, referring to the punch line from the famous commercials.

I taste my Singapore Sling. It isn't perfect, but it's damn close.

"Maybe you could show me around the City sometime."

I glance down at my watch. It's roughly a quarter till eleven. I have a feeling that this is the point where the evening can change gears if I push a little harder. I remind myself that I still have to get up in the morning and go to work, especially since I ran into Teresa tonight. I'd hate to have my business out there if I came in late to work in the morning all disheveled and tired.

While deep in thought, Melody interrupts my thoughts by asking me about my feelings on teaching at TMA.

I gaze into her eyes. She seems genuinely interested in my response. "It's an adjustment, but I'm really digging the newness of it."

She takes another sip of her margarita. "Well, I want to go on record for saying that it's very admirable that a person at your level is giving back to young people."

"You sound like I'm actually somebody important or something."

"Miles," she says coyly. "You can bullshit someone much younger than me, but you have to remember that I know you from way back when, back in those days when you were writing those baby-making songs."

I don't know if it was her blatant and nonchalant use of profanity or her reference to the sensuality of my music, but I'm really feeling her style. For some reason women who are uninhibited tend to put a smile on my face. I guess I've met so many women who put on facades that I have become more increasingly drawn to a woman who puts herself out there for real.

"Did you have a favorite song, Melody?"

"Just one?"

"Flattery will get you everywhere."

She looks upward, as if to ponder the question seriously. "If I had to pick just one, I'd probably go with 'Tonight is Forever.' My girls always say that song is guaranteed to make a woman step out of her panties. I swear, there are times when I've listened to that song and actually felt the baseline pulsing between my thighs."

Whoa.

Let me say that again: Whoa.

It's clear that Melody doesn't believe in wasting time signaling what she wants, and as I sit here across from her with half a Singapore Sling in front of me, I am contemplating tasting her and not that drink.

"I always wanted to know if you guys wrote that song for anyone in particular," she says.

I know I wrote that particular song shortly after Bettina told me that she was pregnant with Travis. Up until that point, the limitations of any kind of relationship we could have were pretty evident by the amount of traveling and the kind of lifestyle I was living as a musician. Truthfully, I didn't expect her to go to term with the pregnancy. I felt like we had connected on a level that would have made her more understanding of my situation. Yeah, I know it's more than a little self-ish, but I felt that her going through with the preg-nancy was her way of trapping me. But being brought up in a strict Bible belt household, I chose to do right by her, so I married her. And to be honest, I loved her. I just don't think that I was ever *in love* with her. We made it work, though, because we wanted Travis to have both of his parents under the same roof. Much to Bettina's credit, she was a very supportive wife, and she did her best to keep peace in the house, and although this might sound like a straight up lie, I bit the bullet and did right by her by never stepping out on her. I didn't look at it as stepping out on her as much as I did stepping out on my son. It's funny how a kid I didn't initially want to have became my pride and joy. But I digress. And sitting across from this beautiful woman right now, I realize that I can't take all of what's on my mind right now into her bedroom tonight.

Digging for the question she asked, I remember and respond, "I don't think we had any inspiration in particular for that song, but if I have to be honest, it was one of my favorite songs, too."

Her eyes widen. "Really?"

"Yes," I say, unable to conceal a smile from having piqued her interest. "Maybe I can show you around on Saturday and you can tell me more about what brought you to this island."

She senses my winding down for the evening and agrees to meet me on Saturday morning at the Columbus Circle entrance to Central Park.

I walk her outside, and after she hails a cab, I tip the driver and give her a hug that lingers even after she releases me.

As I prepare to close her door, I lean over and ask her, "Do you have a dog?"

She looks at me a little confused. "Not any more, but I used to have a Rottweiler. Why do you ask?"

"Just curious," I respond, kissing her gently on her cheek and sending her off into the maze of Manhattan.

6

OCTOBER 22, 2004

JA KENDRICK BROWN

I'm standing outside the Tower Records off 66th and Broadway with Yusef, waiting for Quent. This section of the City's always been laid back. The Upper West Side block we're in is just a few blocks down from Julliard and the Lincoln Center, and other than movie theaters, stores, and the dance studio down the street, the area is pretty much a stack of brownstones.

Quent told us he had to get at us today after school about something real big. I didn't really know what to think because he's not one to just be rah-rah for any ol' reason.

I had to break out the bubble goose down jacket I finally got off lay-a-way because the temp had dropped to the point that a sweatshirt couldn't fight off the cold. My Tims are still unlaced with the tongue stretched out, but I can't bring myself to roll up that one pant leg on my good leg. My little calf would be ashy as hell from all this freeze running up and down these streets. This is one of those days you just have to profile wit your hands in your pockets. I look over at Yusef, and he's even worse off than me.

"Nigga, is that a Union t-shirt up under your sweatshirt?" I ask, just to fuck with him.

"Kid, it's a fucking deep freezer out here." He pulls the hood of his sweatshirt over his skully and starts doing one of those Eminem "8 Mile" running-in-place things to keep warm. "Quent better come on or I'ma have to jet. I got this fine Boriqua mami looking to stroke a nigga later on."

Yusef has a thing for Puerto Rican women and flaunts them like P. Diddy flaunts diamonds. Although he's a deep brown, he likes that light skinned, long hair, "ass so phat that you can see it from the front" thing. Why lock out the sistas though? I asked him once.

"Sistas only speak English."

Man, that's some stupid shit, I thought, but to each his own.

I hope whatever Quent wants to tell us is important enough to push back hustling the trains today. I have Angela in her carrying case leaning against the side of the building with me. Although we know you're not supposed to work the trains the way we do, we've learned how to move around and not get caught. The key is to make it look like you're a music student doing something spontaneous. Sometimes we just skip the "spontaneous" routine and just let everyone know we're trying to make a few ends. It just depends on the time of day and what train we're on.

Just as I'm getting ready to go inside the store to float around and listen to some music, a huge pearl white Cadillac Escalade trimmed in gold pulls up to the corner. The rims are still spinning as the passenger door opens. Quent steps out with a huge grin on his face. I look to see who the driver is, but I don't recognize him. He's a clean-cut brotha with a real nice platinum chain around his neck. The charm on the chain is blinging pretty hard too. He has on a pair of shades, and he's copping that gangsta lean with a Blue Tooth cell phone earpiece in his ear. Around the earpiece I can see he's wearing something like a 2-carat solitaire earring. Nas's "Made You Look" is bumping from the woofers in the truck. He looks over in the general direction of me and Yusef and gives the "what's up" nod. I'm trying not to cheese, but I'm pretty impressed with all of this shit.

Quent daps us up while we're still staring at the ride.

"Yo, hop in," Quent says. "We going for a ride."

"For real?" Yusef says, taking the words right out my mouth.

"Yeah, man. I got a surprise for y'all."

I grab the passenger side backdoor and jump in. The first thing I do is say "fuck the cold" and roll down the window so people can see me up in here. Sometimes I daydream about having a ride like this when I make it big, something like it came off of MTV's "Pimp My Ride." And looking around, I can see that this dude's got TV monitors in the back of the headrests. I look over at Yusef, and he's staring at Gabrielle Union on the screen in front of him. Turning the music down for a minute, the driver stretches his hand over the seat to dap us.

"Terrell Bonds," he says, introducing himself.

"Ja Brown," I say. "And that's Yusef Jackson."

"You guys feel like going over to the studio and hanging out for a bit?"

The backseat is so comfortable that for a moment I realize that I ain't never heard a question so stupid in my life. I would've paid cash money to be sitting in a customized Escalade headed to a recording studio.

"Sure," I respond.

This is all way too much for me, but I close my

eyes and imagine that this is what a brotha like me deserves after the shit I've been through in my life.

WE PULL UP TO A BUILDING BETWEEN 8TH AVENUE and 9th Avenue, a few blocks down from Port Authority. If it wasn't for the parking area behind the building, we'd have been assed-out on getting a space.

"Yo, Quent, how do you know this dude?" Yusef whispers.

We walk inside and stand in the hallway, waiting on the elevator.

"I'll tell you about it when we get up stairs."

We get off on the 7th floor, and the first thing I hear is the music. It's so loud it's beating inside my chest! The lights are pretty low, and down the hall is a door that leads to another room. There's a guy in the room with his back to the door, stretched out over a massive mixing board. Big black leather couches are out in the hallway. A few fine-ass women are walking back and forth in the hall, and I think to myself how cool all of this stuff is.

As Terrell takes us down the hall to what I'm guessing is the producer's booth, I peep a few gold and platinum plaques up and down the walls. I can recognize one of the artists immediately. Standing tall in this big-ass frame with two platinum records is Big Boze's *All In* album. A few years back Big Boze had a song on that album called "You Just Think You Know" that used a sample from this old school group called The Triumphs. Mama had that old Triumph record and used to play it all the time back in the day when she was headed out to those "grown folk" parties. When she was gone, I used to listen to the record myself and look at the artwork on the cover. When I got a little bit older, I actually schooled myself on all of the old school dudes Mama used to listen to. I guess I got my taste in music from her.

"A'ight, son! A'ight, son!" Yusef comments to no one in particular. "Deez niggas is pushing weight up in here. Got the Big Boze joint on the wall and all."

We ease into the producer's booth, and Terrell introduces us to the engineer, a guy named Smoke-T.

"Have a seat," Terrell says to us, as he points at a huge, cushy couch against the wall. "We got this girl group we just signed, and they'll be coming by in a few to lay down some tracks on this joint I'm producing. They call themselves Deja Ice."

I feel like I've heard that name somewhere, like it was in some hip-hop magazine or something as a group to watch out for. I can barely remember hearing the name, 'cause as far as I know, they don't have any joints out there on the radio yet.

We're sitting on the couch kinda spaced out, and Quent leans over and says, "Yo, I seen these shorties! They all dime pieces!"

"How many?" I ask.

"Three, my nigga."

Yusef smiles. "That's the magic number. One for each of us."

We all smile and lean back onto the couch. The beat thumping through the monster speakers is actually *fire*. I guess sitting with it blasting around you makes it sink in a lot quicker.

A few minutes later, Smoke-T turns around in his seat to look down the hall. Everyone looks at the elevator as the doors open and three of the finest girls I've laid eyes on in a minute step out. They all look around our ages, and they're walking our way. Quent leans over grinning and dapping Yusef and me. I can already tell that it's gonna be on and popping up in here. That is unless we got some R. Kelly-ass-nigga trying to block.

Lost in my thoughts, I almost don't notice Terrell standing over us introducing us to the lovely ladies of Deja Ice. That's when I really notice her—the kind of girl who if she breathes on you the right way, you might change religions. Her complexion is the color of milk chocolate, and her hair is pulled back into a ponytail. She has this beautiful smile on her face. Terrell introduces her as Lei Morgan, and I'm relieved because now my angel has a name.

AFTER ALMOST TWO HOURS OF WATCHING DEJA Ice through the recording booth glass, Terrell walks over to us and asks us to come with him. I'd been trying to make eye contact with Lei between takes, and I think I might've succeeded a few times. Though I hate to give up my seat, I follow the others to a room down the hall.

"So what do you think of the setup here?" Terrell asks. He takes a seat behind a nice, expensive-looking desk.

"Well, you know what I think," says Quent. "But let me see what my boys think," he says, looking at Yusef and me.

I'm still trying to figure out what's the connection between Quent and Terrell. I've already figured out that Quent's probably been up in this piece before, so I'm starting to think that maybe Terrell might be interested in signing us as a group or something.

I'm feeling about as nervous as a hooker in church, but the hustler in me is trying to keep the game face going.

"Real nice, " I say, trying to hide my smile. "It's off the chains."

"Thanks," Terrell responds.

Yusef pipes up. "I just appreciate you letting a brotha kick it up in here."

Terrell smiles and decides to cut right to the chase. "I do A & R for Big Business Records. Big Boze is one of our artists."

I'm very familiar with Big Business. I mean, who isn't? They rank up there with Bad Boy, Roc-a-Fella, and Murder Inc. For the last two summers they've had the radios locked with hits.

I'm so amped up I just wanna dap everyone in the room, but I play it cool.

Terrell continues, "I met your boy Quent through one of my partners, and I heard he can blow. He hit me with a little bit of what he can do, but I wanted to have the whole group together to see what I'm really working with."

I look at Quent and nod. I'm glad he didn't leave us out in the cold on this deal like most niggas would.

Terrell continues, "So I just wanted to hear you guys do your thing."

He looks over at me and says, "Ja, I see you got your keyboard with you. Do you think you guys can hit me with a little bit of what you do when you're on the trains?"

"Sure."

Quent, Yusef, and I huddle for a second trying to figure out what to perform. It's not like there's any advance notice, so we're gonna have to shoot straight from the hip.

Yusef tosses out a suggestion. "Why don't we do the original Triumphs' song that Big Boze sampled for 'You Just Think You Know.' What's it called?"

"Tonight is Forever," I say. I know that song like

the back of my hand. Mama always liked that one, too. "Quent, do you know the lyrics?"

"How does the first line go?"

"For so long I've been searching," I say.

"Yeah, I remember it. Let's do it!"

We come out of our huddle, and Terrell nods at us. "You guys got something ready for me?"

"I got you," Quent responds.

I pull out Angela and set my sound for a soft electric piano. Yusef takes his bongos out of his backpack. Within moments, Yusef and I have set a pretty strong groove for Quent to lace.

He starts, "For so long I've been searching for a love like this…."

Terrell sits back in his seat with his arms cocked behind his head. He nods to the beat, smiling. "How old are you guys?" he asks, cutting us off.

"14, 15, and 15," Quent says.

"Damn, that's tight. Ja and Yusef, do you guys sing, too, or are you strictly music?"

"We do background to fill out the three part harmony, but we leave the panty-soaking to Quent," Yusef says.

Terrell laughs. "Yeah, I got you. Let me hear you guys hit the chorus for me right quick so I can see what you guys are working with."

I start playing the section leading into the chorus. Our voices blend together like red beans and rice, and I can tell that we're setting it off in here because Terrell jumps out of his seat and runs down the hall. He rushes back in with Smoke-T. "Do that again, music and all!" he tells us.

We hit it for him again. Now Smoke-T and Terrell are dapping and hopping around like they just discovered gold. I'm starting to get excited my damn self because even I know that if the A & R department is feeling you then you're as good as in there.

Terrell walks over and sits on his desk, facing us. "You guys wouldn't by chance have a demo handy would you?"

We shake our heads "no." If we had a demo, we probably wouldn't be hustling trains, I'm thinking.

"Well, what I'm gonna do is set up a meeting over at our head office and have you sing for Teddy Ray, the CEO. He has to green-light everybody," Terrell says. "I'll just hit Quent on his cell to let you guys know when I need you to come through."

Quent, Yusef, and I are dapping each other while we pack up our things.

As we step toward the elevator to leave out, I see Lei and the other sisters from Deja Ice chilling in the lobby. I walk over to her and extend my hand. She takes it, smiling.

"It was a pleasure meeting you," I say. It's the only thing that I can muster up the nerve to say.

"It was nice meeting you too," she responds.

"Hopefully I'll see you around sometime."

"That would be nice," she responds. Her hand gently slides away from mine as the elevator doors open and I step on.

WE BREAK OUT A LITTLE AFTER 6. WE OPT TO HIT the trains headed to Harlem so we can pick up a few extra dollars on the way home. We might be rich one day, but that day ain't today.

We hit the tunnel between Port Authority and Times Square and play that for a few minutes before we hop the A train, headed Uptown. As we settle into our space and

Quent gives the preliminary speech about how we're just some students trying to do something positive with our music, I notice this guy sitting toward the middle of the car. He's leaning against the rail by the door. He looks mad familiar too, but I can't place him. He has this baldie haircut, but he looks kinda important. Then it hits me! I almost didn't recognize him without the Afro, but I'm almost convinced that's Miles Thompson over there. It'd only make sense, since we just got through doing one of the 'Triumphs' songs a few minutes ago.

I nudge Quent and say, "Yo, let's hit that 'Tonight is Forever' again."

They're probably thinking that I just wanna celebrate Big Business being interested and whatnot, but I'm really thinking more bout that tip we could get if that really is Miles Thompson over there.

I'm starting to second-guess myself, but we start the song up anyway.

The way I see it, there's nothing to lose, but everything to gain.

7

OCTOBER 22, 2004

MILES THOMPSON

This morning I awoke to find my sheets soaked with sweat. I flipped the pillow over to the dry side, but I couldn't relax enough to go back to sleep. I am totally exhausted by these nightmares. I've barely had a few nights of restful sleep in this apartment. I'm seriously contemplating going to see another psychologist.

I got up from my bed and put on music by my namesake, Miles Davis. *Kind of Blue* filled the room, as I sat on the edge of my bed looking at Travis's picture. I dressed for work and went in early as usual. Teresa hadn't arrived yet. She must have had a late night herself.

The day finally started to move along when Melody called me around noon to remind me of our date tomorrow. I plan to get my mind together before we go out so I can really focus on her this time.

By the afternoon, classes were flowing and the kids seemed to be genuinely interested in the day's lesson. I played "A Night in Tunisia", and for many of them it was their first time hearing it. When I showed them pictures of Dizzy and Bird, they got a kick out of Dizzy's puffed-out cheeks.

"Mr. Thompson, why is his face like that?" one of the kids had asked.

"That's the way he would blow up his cheeks when he played."

Another kid chimed in. "Mr. James, my trumpet teacher, says you're not supposed to blow with your cheeks out like that when you play."

"Well, technically you're not supposed to, but Dizzy had muscle tissue damage and had to blow like that," I responded.

One of the kids in the back of the classroom asked, "What is that he's playing? That doesn't even look like a trumpet!"

"Well, Dizzy had an accident with his horn once, and it got bent out of shape. He liked the altered tone of it so much that he later had his trumpets made with the bell coming straight up. Remember, he had his own way of doing things," I said.

"That song sounds crazy. How did they come up with something like that?" another kid asked.

"My guess is that when you get two very talented and creative musicians together, these types of things happen."

These kids are way too bright. This is definitely the part of my job that keeps me on my toes: the questions.

The two students for my private lessons today had to cancel, so I caught the train down to Greenwich Village to check out this small record shop I had read about in *The Village Voice*. I still like to go to independent record stores and pick up music I can't get anywhere else. I picked up a CD of a cat named Chestnut Coley. I see where he covered an old Earth, Wind & Fire track that I used to like.

I always like to hear what these youngsters do with our music. If an artist remakes a song from scratch without changing the overall composition, they can record it without permission from the publisher or songwriter. I still get paid, but a lot of times I don't know who's covering the songs until after they're already in the store and The Harry Fox Agency sends me a check. Every blue moon I hear a cover of one of my songs that sounds better than the original, and at times like that, I'm glad that I had anything to do with the song at all. It's really nice to see people build on what was once a melody hummed in the shower or the car and put their own little twist on it.

Now samples, that's a very different matter. I get to approve those, and even then I try not to let just anyone sample my music. Out of all of the requests that I've received through my music co-publisher, I've only accepted two of them. And that's mainly because those two kids came to me personally and pleaded their cases. Some of my music peers will let any tom, dick, and thug sample their music just for a paycheck. It's almost like they don't look at what they have created as art so they don't mind other people pissing on it. I don't see anything wrong with letting kids sample your music to rap to, but I'd rather the lyrics not be violent or misogynistic.

Tired from walking around, I decide to head on back to the apartment to fix a little dinner and map out my date with Melody tomorrow. Stepping into the subway station, I grab a copy of *TimeOut New York* and head down the stairs to the platform to wait for the Uptown A train.

AS I TAKE A SEAT NEAR THE MIDDLE DOOR OF THE middle car, I lean my head back and close my eyes. I feel the express train moving rapidly, but in my mind I am still. My eyes are so tired I leave them closed.

I think about the play last night. While reconstructing Melody's beauty in my mind, I keep stopping at Teresa. Maybe it's just me, but it seems like her temperature changed slightly when Melody came up to join us. That doesn't make any sense though, especially since Teresa's husband was standing right there. I'm pretty famous for misreading women, so I'll just chalk that random thought up to my bad judgment. But the fact that Teresa didn't come in early this morning makes me wonder. I can't let myself dwell on that though. Teresa is married, and while I might have made a move in my younger days, having had a family of my own, I can't see making a fool out of another man like that.

I ease my mind back to Melody, back to someone I can safely fantasize about. Just as I remember the feeling of her leg brushing against mine in the theater, the train comes to a stop at Port Authority. As people step into the car, I notice three kids positioning themselves at the front of the car. A kid with a red Afro steps in front of the others and begins to speak.

"Ladies and gentlemen, we'll only take a moment of your time to share with you the gifts God has given us. We're just young students trying to follow our dreams and keep out of trouble...."

The other two are pulling out instruments. The one with dreads is pulling a keyboard out of a bag. The other shorter kid with the low haircut is taking some bongos out of his backpack. They seem to be quite a little ensemble for their ages. They look as if they could be around the same age as Travis.

As the kid in front finishes, the one with the dreadlocks starts playing, and I can recognize the tune immediately. I should—because I wrote it. These kids are tackling "Tonight is Forever" on a swaying express train. I'm impressed so I give them my undivided attention.

The singer has quite a voice on him. Terry Jacobs, the guy who originally sang lead on that song, would be impressed. I'm impressed by the kid on the keyboards, too, because he's playing all of the subtle nuances of the music, the kind you don't get from the manufactured sheet music they sell in record shops. I smile because I know that there are probably only a handful of kids out there who have even heard the original version of this song. To be honest, when the music started, I half expected the kid with the red Afro to start rapping.

Just as I start nodding my head with the music, the lead singer walks over toward me and starts singing the chorus. Everyone in the car starts looking at me now, and I hear a voice from somewhere mumble, "That's Miles Thompson from The Triumphs. He wrote that song." (It seems like there's always some music buff lurking nearby.) Now it seems that all of the attention of the train is on these three kids and me. The one with the dreadlocks eases his keyboard down the aisle as he positions it at an angle where I can see him play. Immediately he launches into a solo with his right hand, his left hand balancing the keyboard. I watch his fingers move nimbly up and down the keyboard, breaking down and reconstructing my chords. This kid looks like he's been taking piano lessons his entire life.

As the kids wrap up the song, everyone begins to applaud. The kids take a bow and point at me.

"Ladies and gentlemen, Mr. Miles Thompson!" the kid with the dreadlocks says, pointing at me.

I'm blushing now. Not because I'm embarrassed by the attention, but I just feel a weird sense of accomplishment just being recognized for any contribution to what those kids just did. They were absolutely awesome! People in the car clap for me, and I can hear a woman's voice say, "I told you it was him."

The kids take out a cap and begin walking along the train for tips. When they get to me, I place a twenty into the hat. "That's was pretty good, guys," I say.

"Thank you, sir," they respond, almost in unison.

And like that, they are moving their act to the next car.

As I watch them walk out of the car, I smile. A blur of memories rush through my head, as I suddenly remember the smell of the recording studio and the feel of those tight, shiny clothes we wore onstage. I can feel the dampness of the sheets moments after Bettina made love to me for the first time. I can feel my baby son sleeping peacefully in my arms, only a few hours after he was delivered. You never know what kind of memories music can stir up.

With the melody of the song still flowing through my head, I realize that this is one of those sweet moments and that the kids' performance was exactly what I needed without even knowing it.

8

OCTOBER 22, 2004

JA KENDRICK BROWN

We did a'ight on the trains today, considering we didn't really hustle all that long. It was cool as hell playing that song for Miles Thompson though. We really milked it. I don't think we've ever gotten a response like that before. The money from the few cars we played on was pretty strong, too. Add that up with Terrell wanting to sign us to a record deal, and I had a pretty good day. I get off the train feeling like a seven figga nigga.

Approaching my block, my heart drops in my chest.

There it is.

Big and bold as shit.

The forest green Hummer.

I feel stupid because I'd gotten used to not seeing him over the last few weeks. I guess I was hoping he had gotten arrested or shot or something. Now here he is. I brace myself and start climbing the stairs to the apartment.

When I insert my key and twist open the door, I come face-to-face with the barrel of a gun. I freeze, scared as shit.

"Oh, it's you," Daryl says, lowering his nine-millimeter. "Little nigga, you better knock before you come up in here like that."

I step into the dark apartment as my sister's naked boyfriend walks back to the bedroom, closing the door behind him. I stand by the door for a moment, still paralyzed. The only light is coming from the bathroom, and the door is open. That fool likes to have some kind of light on when he's here, I guess so he can see anyone sneaking up on him.

I finally walk over to the couch and prop Angela up against the wall. My heart is beating like a motherfucker. I inhale and exhale slowly, trying to get myself calm. When I finally settle down, I can actually hear Sherita and Daryl in the back room fucking. This nigga nearly killed me, and now he's back there fucking my sister. For a moment I just want to run back there and stab him or something. But I can't. He's supposed to be a pretty big time drug lord up here, and I just feel like he would kill both my sister and me if everything went to shit.

For nearly a year, I have sat back and watched this nigga take over the apartment my mother raised me and my sister in, using it like some kind of secret "Batcave." About three months ago, I got into a fight with him over my sister getting high, and he almost choked me to death on the kitchen table. After that, I'd just bail out whenever he came over. I can't begin to count all the nights I spent riding the train just to find a place to sleep.

The whole situation is embarrassing as hell. I ain't even told Yusef or Quent about any of this. They're my boys and all, but they got one perception of me, and I don't know if I trust anyone to know this other side. No one's caught on to what I've been doing, and to be honest, I don't think my sister's been sober long enough to realize that I'm hardly ever here anymore.

I walk into the bathroom, close the door, and look into the mirror. I still look jarred. My dreads fall down past my shoulders. My chin is starting to sprout some fuzz. My mustache is starting to get a little darker, too. My skin is clear, and I look clean. I smile at the mirror just to see a change in my facial expression, and my lips peel back into a wide grin. As I look at myself, I feel my cheeks catch and hold my smile there, and I realize that I'm smiling for real.

I can hear music in my mind. I can hear all of these melodies like a whirlwind, and I run back to grab my notebook off of the bookshelf in the main room. I close the door to the bathroom and sit down on the toilet lid with my pen in hand. I draw five quick lines and put a treble clef on the left side. Above the staff I begin writing the names of chords and then I start putting a melody on the staff, note by note. Before I realize it, my head is bopping to the melody that I'm writing. Quickly, I draw another five lines beneath that staff to do my bass part.

I don't even realize how long I have been writing until Daryl barges into the bathroom, dick swinging. "Nigga, I gotta piss. Get the fuck up."

I jump up and leave out the bathroom, like I was up in his space as opposed to him being up in mine. Just as I walk away, something in me makes me turn around and head back. I feel as if I don't check this nigga on dissing me, he'll just think I'm some punk bitch who'll roll over when he asks me to. He had already pulled a gun on me tonight, but it's like I don't wanna remember that part.

"What the fuck do you want, l'il nigga?" he says.

"My name is Ja Kendrick," I say. "Not L'il Nigga. And I don't think you should come around here no more."

"What?" he asks, like he don't understand what I'm

saying. "Nigga, fuck you! You betta take yo bitch ass to sleep before I stomp yo heart out."

He pushes me really hard, but the wall breaks my fall. I can feel the pain shooting through my shoulder blades, and it hurts like hell.

"Yo, man, why does it have to be like this?" I ask. "You know this shit is wrong. What you're doing is just wrong. Straight up. If you're gonna do this, at least leave me and my sister out of it."

He steps over to me and puts his finger dead in the center of my chest. I can feel him poking my sternum, and my heart starts to race a mile a minute. With his other hand he hits me in my stomach, knocking me to the floor. My whole body is hurting as he stands over me.

"I should kill yo dumb ass. Don't you ever, *ever* swell up on me like you wanna do something! I will end you, nigga. I don't give a fuck if you Sherita's brotha or not. Try me like that again and yo ass'll be six feet under this bitch."

He turns around and walks back into my sister's bedroom and closes the door.

I slowly push myself off the floor. I get so angry my face gets hot, and I can feel a tear roll down my cheek. I imagine kicking down that door and killing him, but then I start to wonder what if I'm not quick enough or strong enough to get him before he gets me?

I reach over and pick up my notebook off the floor. I walk over to Angela and then decide that I'll come back for her sometime on Monday. I open the closet by the door and grab my emergency backpack, the one I keep packed with everything that I'll need for a few days.

As I head for the door, I find myself staring at my sister's bedroom door. Part of me thinks, "Fuck it. I'd rather die than be a punk bitch in my own crib." The other part of me thinks about Mama and how she felt I was destined to do something bigger and better. She wouldn't want me to throw it all away on a fool like Daryl. I open the door and lock it behind me. It's a little after midnight, and it's cold as a motherfucker outside, but I know that the train station is only a few blocks away, and it's pretty warm in there.

As I'm walking I catch myself singing under my breath. "For so long I've been searching for a love like this." I think back to earlier in the day, and I see Lei Morgan's face. I can still feel her touch tingling on my hand. The rage in me starts to give way to this warm feeling, the feeling that things are gonna get better for me real soon. I slide my Metro card through the slot on the turnstile and take a seat on a wooden bench, as I shake my dreads across my face to hide while I catch a few Z's before the train comes.

OCTOBER 23, 2004

MILES THOMPSON

The silver globe across the street from the Columbus Circle entrance to Central Park sparkles in the morning sunlight. Next to the globe, standing like a giant, is Trump Plaza. I sit down on a bench couched beneath the broad branches of the park's trees and glance down at my watch. I'm fifteen minutes early for my date with Melody.

During last night's brief phone conversation, we agreed to meet up at 10 a.m. and just see where the day took us. I encouraged her to dress for comfort. The temperature is in the low forties, but the sun is high in the sky. It feels like it's going to be a beautiful day.

I see her out the corner of my eye in a red bubble down jacket and a matching toboggan. She looks too cute in her jeans and running shoes. If her age was difficult to notice the other night, it is almost impossible to notice today because she could easily be in her late twenties or early thirties.

"Melody," I say, standing and waiving my hands to draw her attention.

She smiles and walks toward me. As we embrace, I feel the warmth of her body through her jacket.

"Hi, Miles," she says, smiling. "I see that I'm dealing with a punctual brother."

"Habit of an Ellison-Wright man."

"Oh, you're an Ellison-Wright man? I really shouldn't be surprised. After all, you fit the bill to a tee."

"What's that supposed to mean?" I ask, playing along.

She lifts an eyebrow and looks at me mockingly. "They say you can always tell a Ellison-Wright man, but you can't tell him much."

"Touché," I respond as we both laugh.

"Seriously," she says. "One of my nephews just graduated from Ellison-Wright this past May. We're really proud of him."

"That's great. What's he doing now?"

"First year at Johns Hopkins Medical School."

We begin walking east down the broad sidewalks of 59th Street, Central Park a picturesque scene of natural beauty to our left, extreme upscale hotels to our right directly across the street.

"What brought you to the City?" I ask.

As she walks, her body sways gently from side to side, the way that a teenage girl's body would sway while holding the stuff animal her boyfriend won for her down at Coney Island. She glances over at me, responding, "I've been working for this company based out of Manhattan doing event planning. I was in their New Jersey office. After I got divorced, I decided that I needed a change of scenery and my company had an opening in the home office."

"You didn't think about just moving to another location, like Dallas or Atlanta?"

"Well, to be honest, I've always wanted to live in Manhattan, and I'm very happy with my company, so I didn't really want to live anywhere else." She looks down and nudges me playfully with her elbow. "So what brought you to New York? Aren't you a Southern boy?"

I chuckle. "Born and bred in the wilds of Mississippi.""So why New York?"

I pause for a moment weighing my response. "I guess, just like you, I needed a fresh start."

Once we reach Fifth Avenue, we turn right and begin walking south. Upscale department store awnings frame the street on either side.

I point up and down the streets. "This is the outdoor mall for the extremely wealthy…"

"…and those who want to act like they are!"

We laugh. I hadn't expected her to be so animated. By this time I'm realizing just how far off I was about my presumptions of her the last time we met.

"You don't really need a tour of this City, do you?" I ask playfully.

"Can I be honest with you?"

"Sure."

"No, I don't really need a tour of the City," she says smiling.

The joke is on me. I smile and pull her closer to me. "I was thinking anyone who lived this close to New York should have already figured out how to get around it."

She looks up at me while reaching her arms around my waist. "Can I be honest with you again?"

"Sure," I say, relaxing in her embrace. I feel as if we're finally cutting to the chase.

"I just wanted to spend a day with you. I really enjoyed myself the other night. I just wanted to see what it would feel like to spend more time with you."

"So?"

"So what?"

"So how does it feel?" I ask.

"So far, so good, Miles. No complaints here."

"I have to watch you. You're smooth," I say, as we continue down Fifth Avenue.

———

AFTER HAVING AN EARLY LUNCH AT A SMALL, quaint Greek restaurant in the East Village, we enjoy a nice stroll over to a photography exhibit at NYU. The sun is pushing back all of the clouds, and its warmth and light are nice additions to the cool air. Although it's our second date in this part of the City, it feels different this time.

"I love the fall, Miles."

"Oh really? Why?"

"The very first time I fell in love was in the fall."

"There must be a story behind that."

"Well," she says. "Back when I was in college—I was a freshman, I think—I was so in love with this guy named Charles. I was eighteen, and I had never been away from home before, and I was scared. Then he came along."

"What happened to him?"

In a matter-of-fact tone, she says, "He cheated on me, just like every other guy. Back then, I told myself that I deserved better so I left him. But the way he made me feel was incredible. I guess the memory is pretty bittersweet, though. I still find myself getting that giddy feeling when the fall rolls around."

I wonder why she's telling me all of this, but I sense that she's just a very open person. "You said that you felt you deserved better back then. You don't feel the same way now?"

"I don't know. I've just learned to accept a lot less. After my divorce I came to the conclusion that most men are incapable of being faithful."

"That's a pretty major statement."

"Yeah, I know. But that's been my experience. All of my girlfriends who are single have convinced me that I should just take each date for what it's worth and tend to my own needs."

"Is that what this is? Us, I mean."

She pauses, as if she's said too much. "I didn't go into this thinking that way, but I'm a realist. You're a sexy man, and I know you probably have a lot of women throwing themselves at you. I'd be cool just getting to spend time with you when time permitted. That is unless you're not interested."

"So far so good, Melody. No complaints here," I say.

Part of me is flattered by her previous remark; the other part is somewhat disturbed though. I haven't been around a woman as fun and interesting as Melody in quite a while, and the idea that she has all but given up on finding something real, something that she can hold on to, is throwing me for a loop.

We make a left at Washington Park and head onto the campus. The afternoon is still young, but I've already committed myself to spending the day with Melody.

Earlier in the week, between classes, I read an article in the Village Voice about a young artist named Marques Donovan who has a photography exhibit at NYU for the next two weeks. Only 27 years old, he is already being heralded as the next Herb Ritts. Honestly, I barely remembered the exhibit was still going on. Melody has never heard of him, but that doesn't stop us from enjoying his series of striking black and white nude photographs.

After an hour of checking out the exhibit, we decide to continue on.

"That was nice," Melody says.

I smile. The statement sounds loaded, since many of the shots were very sensual in nature. Not coincidentally, Marques named the collection "The Voyeur Series."

Then just as we turn the corner headed back toward Union Square, our fingers gravitate and interlock. Up until that point, she had just held on to my arm as if I were her formal escort. When our fingers touch, warmth spreads throughout my body. Because I am a keyboardist, my fingers are pretty sensitive, so the act of holding hands is very intimate to me. We look at each other and smile.

"So," I start, glancing into her eyes, secretly hoping that we won't trek too far across the City by foot. "What would you like to do now?"

"Why don't we go back to my place, and I can make us some cocoa."

"That sounds nice."

"And Miles, we should probably catch a cab. My feet are starting to hurt."

I smile. This woman is batting a thousand.

WHEN WE REACH MELODY'S PLACE ON THE UPPER West Side, I notice that her apartment is roughly the size of mine. She invites me in, and I take a seat on the couch in the den. The first things I notice are the art prints and bookshelves that adorn the apartment. Everything is laid out efficiently using all of the available space, and yet there's a very soft, feminine tone to the place.

I glance around the room, admiring her interior

decorating skills, while the smooth sounds of Earth, Wind & Fire's "Love's Holiday" float from small speakers in the upper corners of the room.

"Nice selection," I say as she hands me a glass of chilled White Zinfandel.

She sits down next to me on the sofa with her glass in hand. "To making a new friend," she says raising her glass.

"To making a new friend," I repeat clicking my glass against hers.

I take a cool sip and smile.

"Why the smile?" she asks as one spreads across her own face.

"This day has been really nice."

"I know."

Before my glass is empty, Melody refills it. So much for cocoa, I tell myself.

For a moment I chuckle at the thought of whether she's trying to get me drunk, but when I finish the second glass, she doesn't immediately go to refill it. Instead she asks me if I'd like another. I nod because I think I can get away with another glass or two before I truly get a buzz going.

From the sofa I can see the shadows of the sunset against the side of the building across the street. Within the next half hour, it will be dark outside. I sip my drink slowly, as Melody asks if I'm comfortable.

"I'm good."

"Any more Zinfandel?"

"No thank you," I respond. "I'm good for now."

"OK," she says rising to her feet.

She starts to stand up too quickly and loses her balance, falling forward. I catch her as she falls on me.

"Ooh," she says, surprised that she fell. "I'm glad I have a good man to catch me."

Her eyes look at me, and for the first time I sense just how seductive this woman can be, and I like it.

"A good man can come in handy." My eyes are locked into hers completely.

"Yes," she says, returning my gaze, her body still stretched across mine. "A good man would never take advantage of a woman who is helpless."

I nod.

She continues, "Helpless to his sexiness, to his touch, to his voice."

"A good man wouldn't do that," I say breathlessly.

"You're a good man aren't you, Miles?"

By now our voices are whispers.

"Yes, I am."

"And you wouldn't take advantage of me," she says, inching her lips closer to mine.

"Of course not," I say. "Unless you wanted me to."

"You mean unless I wanted you to do this," she says, kissing me deeply on my lips.

"Yes," I whisper, as her teeth tug lightly at my bottom lip.

Her kiss pulls me in, and I feel my hands wrap around her body, massaging her shoulders softly. I feel the tension from her body release as her body settles into mine. Her tongue dances in my mouth like an extinguisher seeking to put out a fire. I match her intensity with my own, easing my hands slowly down her back in smooth slow circles, finally resting them firmly on her behind. She moans into my mouth and lifts herself up, pulling my face into the crevice of her neck where my tongue continues dancing against her sweet, golden skin.

"That's nice," she moans while massaging my scalp with her delicate fingers. I can feel the nerves in my head tickle from her touch, and my entire body becomes erotically charged.

Moving my hands upward, I slide her shirt up, my fingers dancing up and down her exposed flesh in massaging motions, as if her body were a grand piano. She raises her hands above her head allowing me to slide her shirt off. As I take in the splendid view of her sculpted body, she positions herself atop me. I quickly unfasten her bra, raising my body so that her right nipple falls gently into my mouth. I cup it with my left hand while massaging the pressure points in her back with my right hand. She falls back against me and I have only my right hand to support me as she grinds her hips into mine.

As my tongue swirls around her other nipple, she pushes me down on my back and slides my shirt up. Within moments we are lying together naked, kisses moving slowly across each other's body.

"I want to feel you inside of me," Melody whispers. "Do you have a condom?"

At the sound of her voice, I feel my manhood pulsing, longing to feel the heat of her body stroking me. I didn't realize that we would find ourselves in this position today, but I planned ahead anyway because I didn't want to be caught totally off guard. I reach over and pull a condom out of my jacket pocket and roll it on.

Just as I get situated, Melody rises from the couch, taking me by the hand. She leads me into her bedroom, and my eyes lock on the mountainous king size bed that seems to fill the room. I follow her, my erection throbbing, as she pulls back the fluffy comforter and lies upon her back.

"Come here," she says, as I approach her.

I lie down, parting her legs as she plants kisses along my chest. I enter her, and for a moment I am totally lost in the warmth and wetness of her body. I look into her eyes and she smiles as she moans. Our bodies move as one, as if engaging in some kind of preor-dained choreography.

As we change positions I taste the saltiness of her skin with my kisses. Sweat drips down her chest, down between her breasts and onto her firm stomach. With each thrust our movements become more powerful. She pushes into me with such force that I feel as if I will explode. I pull her into me and our movements accelerate. Between her rapid breaths and my own, we lose ourselves completely in ecstasy.

Just as her moans crescendo, I feel myself ex-ploding in an incredible orgasm. She feels me pulsing and pushes into me matching my gasps with her own screams.

Wiping away the sweat that's running into my eyes, I look at her. She looks absolutely perfect reclined upon the sheets, body flawlessly fit and smooth. She looks at me, a breathless smile upon her lips.

"Wonderful," I say. My baritone voice pierces a quietness that was only moments ago punctuated by moans and gasps.

"Yes. Very wonderful."

I pull her close to me, and she rests her head upon my chest. Her scent intoxicates me, and her cool body, drying from the perspiration, warms against me.

Placing a hand on my chest, she looks up at me. "I really enjoyed today."

"Baby," I say, before realizing just how comfortable I have become. "The day is not over yet."

10

OCTOBER 24, 2004

JA KENDRICK BROWN

Yusef is 100% straight up Brooklyn personified. I bullshitted yesterday away hanging out with that knucklehead in Bed Stuy. I gotta admit that I'm probably a lot closer to Yusef than Quent. The funny thing is that I met Yusef through Quent.

Because we all live in different boroughs, we were never at the same school. I met Quent back in the sixth grade when he wound up standing next to me at the Puerto Rican Day parade. Because he was light skinned, I assumed he was Puerto Rican. We traded words back and forth, blah-zay skip, and he ended up inviting me to a block party later on that night.

I met Yusef at that same party. I guess what I liked about him the most was that he was funny as hell. Nigga had me straight cracking up that night. Even now, he still trips me out with the stuff he says. I'm convinced that comedy is his true calling. He's one of the few people I know who can be consistently funny whether he's telling a joke or just saying some everyday shit.

It's not that I don't like hanging out with Quent, 'cause I do, but after the kind of night I had Friday, I needed to just be around someone who is more prone to look at the lighter side of things, someone who could make me feel better. Plus, Quent had told us he would be in Jersey for the entire weekend visiting his father anyway and wouldn't be back until late Sunday night.

I ended up crashing at Yusef's crib Saturday night, which, unbeknownst to him, saved me from having to ride the trains all night again. We talked about what it would be like when we got rich doing this music thing. His bottom line was this: he and some dime piece would have two little shorties, live out in Long Island in a phat crib and have a 500 series Benz sitting on 24 inch chrome dubs.

I told him that I just wanted to get a new house for my sister and me, one where maybe we each had our own wings of the house.

"You can do that with the money we'll get."

I nodded. "I hope so."

This morning he told me that he had to go see his grandmother in Jamaica, Queens, so I decided to let him take care of his business and come on back to The City to see if I could get a few minutes of practice in at a keyboard store, since Angela is back at my sister's crib and I don't plan to go back there until tomorrow.

The hawk is not bad as I walk down and catch the 3 train back to Times Square. I like walking past all the huge skyscrapers down here. I imagine some big deals are going down in them, the kind of mega-deals that could change the entire game.

As I leave the train station at 42nd Street and walk out into an ocean of tourists, I think about my life and realize that something has to change. I wonder how I can get my sister straight, get her clean 'cause right now she's a wreck. How do I get Daryl out of my sister's life? How do I make something happen with this music? I know Big Business Records is interested, but a lot of people talk noise. I know that I can't afford to get too amped on that until there's a real offer on the table. I wonder when I'll see Lei Morgan again. How can I break free of all the drama?

I look at the Bertelsmann building as I pass the corner of 45th and Broadway. A limousine pulls up, and I strain to see who steps out. Nobody that I can recognize, so I push on.

I walk up a few blocks and bust a right on 48th Street, headed to Sam Ash, my favorite music spot on this side of town. They have a keyboard room on the side closed off from the rest of the store, so every once and a while I'll come down to the spot and practice.

"What's up, Akil?" I say, walking through the door.

"Ja! Whassup, young?" Akil says, stepping out from behind the counter and dapping me. "I ain't seen you in a minute."

Akil is huge and black as a motherfucker, like a mountain or something, but he's real mellow. He might scare the hell out of some people because of his size, but he's harmless when you get know him. Just a bass player holding down a day job—at least that's what he told me one day after I'd practiced for about half the day.

"Yeah, you know I'm just trying to keep up with school, music and all."

I hand him my backpack, and he hands me a claim ticket to pick it up when I get ready to leave the store.

"Anyone in there?" I ask.

"Naw, not really, kid. Go on and do your thing."

"Thanks."

I stroll past several keyboard displays, headed to the performance room. I walk through the door into the closed off section, and there are about six electric pianos and a real baby grand situated around the room. I take a seat at the baby grand. The two doors in the room are closed, so I don't have to worry about distracting folks out front.

When my fingers fall on the keys, I feel this glow come over my soul. I don't care how much fancy shit these new keyboards can do. You just can't fake the feel of real piano keys beneath your fingertips. And to me, the sound is different. More real.

For a minute I just start playing different chords in a rhythm, just to hear the richness of the sounds. I close my eyes. I ain't playing anything in particular, but I'm aware of the melody. I think about all the things going on in my world. I think about how much I miss Mama and how much I want to help my sister. My chords start sounding sad, and I play much slower.

Then I think about hanging out with Quent and Yusef, us working the trains. I think about how excited Terrell Bonds and Smoke-T were when we did our thing over at the studio. I think about how cool it would be playing for the CEO of the label. I think about Lei Morgan and the feel of her soft hand before I left the studio. My fingers begin to move faster. I feel the music brighten, my chords dancing up and down the piano. I feel like I'm outside of my body and my fingers are just moving all over the place. For a quick moment, I imagine Bugs Bunny scooping up the keys of the piano in that old cartoon and slinging them down one by one. My fingers are on fire. I feel like I'm connected to the piano, and the music is looping back and forth between me and the piano like a figure eight infinity sign or something. When I finally open my eyes, I realize I'm not alone.

***

MILES THOMPSON AND THIS FINE ASS WOMAN ARE leaning against the piano, listening to everything I'm playing. They catch me off guard, and I just stop cold. I wonder how long they were standing there.

"Hey, young brother. Didn't mean to interfere with your playing. I just heard you and wanted to come back and listen for minute," he says.

"Uh, no problem," I manage. I'm buggin' out 'cause this is Miles Thompson peeping my skills.

"You're the guy from the train, aren't you? The one who was grooving with that group the other day."

I'm surprised that he even remembers me, but I nod, not really sure what to say.

"You have some really interesting combinations going on there. How long have you been playing?"

"Since I was about six."

He rocks back, as if he's impressed. "How old are you now?"

"Fifteen," I say.

"So, you've been taking piano lessons for about nine years?"

"Actually, I ain't never taken piano lessons."

"Oh, really?" he says, looking back at the woman standing with him. They both seem tickled as hell.

"So you do all of this by ear?"

"No, I can read music. I taught myself to read and write back when I was little."

He laughs again. "Man, I'm really impressed. You're very talented."

"Thanks," I say. I'm cheesing because no one would ever believe that I was getting these kinds of props from a music legend.

Miles sits down at the keyboard next to mine and starts playing it. I expect him to start up a Triumph song, but he starts hitting a bunch of crazy-ass chords. For a second, I can't catch on to what he's doing.

"Play along," he calls out over the music. "Follow me. See where I'm going with this."

I listen for a minute, and I start to hear the chords. It's like he's playing the two most dissonant notes out of a five-note chord. I find the key that he's playing in and start to solo on my piano in the same key. I skip around, chording the same partial chords with my left hand. He starts banging his keys harder and calls out a key change. "E flat seven!"

I change it up and continue the vamp he's started. Beyond the sound of my piano I can hear Miles Thompson ripping it like it ain't nobody's business. I had no idea that he was that nice on the piano. Most peeps can't fuck with jazz, especially if they come from a structured type of music like R&B, so he's on a whole other level as far as I'm concerned.

After playing for a few minutes, we wrap it up.

"Not bad," he says. "Not bad at all. Not many people can hang with the stylings of Thelonius Monk."

"I didn't know," I say surprised. "I ain't really heard a lot of his stuff."

"That's cool. Well, if you ever want to hear any jazz or just practice your chops on another piano, feel free to give me a call or drop through over at the Thelonius Monk Academy. I'm a music teacher over there. I'm usually there until 4:30 or 5 in the evening."

He hands me a card with his info.

"By the way, this is Melody Lithcott," he says, stepping out of the way so I can see the fine ass sista beside him a little better.

"Nice to meet you," I say, standing to shake her hand. Mama had always told me to stand when greeting a woman.

"Nice to meet you, too. You're very talented," she responds. "You and Miles should really get together sometime."

I want to say the she and *I* should get together sometime, but I keep that joke to myself.

"What's your name?" Miles Thompson asks me.

Oh yeah. My name. Almost forgot. "Ja—Ja Kendrick Brown. My friends call me 'Ja.'"

"Well, Ja, it was nice meeting you, and I look forward to hearing from you sometime soon."

"Most definitely," I say, as he extends his hand, dapping me like he was one of my boys. "Most definitely."

I'm grinning non-stop as I hand Akil my claim ticket and pick up my backpack. I step out into the cool air and start to walk back toward Broadway when I see an Escalade that looks like Terrell Bonds's. It's headed north, and for a second I see a fat yellow dude in the passenger seat who looks like Quent. I start running toward the corner, but by the time I get there the Escalade is already down the street, almost out of view.

I hope I didn't just see what I think I did.

If that was Quent, what's the deal with him saying he'd be at his father's crib in Jersey until later tonight? But an even more fucked-up thought comes to mind: what reason would Quent have right now to hang out with Terrell Bonds without me and Yusef there?

THE SECOND MOVEMENT

11

OCTOBER 25, 2004

MILES THOMPSON

I'm stretched out on the recliner, stomach full from our lasagna dinner, and Bettina's nestled up on the couch with her crossword puzzles. I have no idea of what's on the television because I'm absorbed in this article in Black Enterprise. *Just a typical Friday night.*

I glance over at Bettina. She runs her fingers through her low cut Halle Berry do, as she studies her puzzle book. At first I was bothered about it because I felt she should've consulted me before she went and chopped off all of her hair. After all, I'm her husband. I mean, I wouldn't just go and cut off all of my hair when I know she likes my hair, but obviously she didn't feel the same when she cut off the hair that used to brush against her shoulder blades. Part of me is still upset with her, but she does look kind of nice with a fresh look. I'm not going to tell her that though.

"Miles, honey," she says. I can already tell that she's going to ask me to do something because she only uses the word "honey" when she needs something done.

"Yes," I respond.

"Can you go in the kitchen and bring me one of those V8 Splashes?"

I know that I shouldn't snap, but we haven't had sex in nearly six months, and everything rises to the surface so quickly that I can't stop it. "I'm busy right now," I respond. "Something wrong with your feet?"

"See, this is the kind of shit I'm talking about!" she starts.

I know that I'm starting this fight, but I can't seem to stop myself from twisting the dagger. It's like I'm fed up with all of this stupid shit in my marriage, and now is the time the pressure blows the cap off the tank.

"What shit? Huh?" I raise my own voice.

"I ask you to do something simple, something that any normal husband would do for his wife, and all you can do is give me shit over it."

I'm surprised at how fast the anger grows inside of me. "So now I'm not normal, huh?"

"I don't know why I'm surprised. You don't ever really listen to what I say. You always have to twist things around."

Frustrated I go into the kitchen and get the V8 Splash out of the refrigerator. I place it firmly down on the coffee table in front of her. "Satisfied?"

"I don't even want it now!"

I plop down in the recliner and grab the magazine. "See? All of this is bullshit."

"Why are you with me if you think our marriage is bullshit then?"

I don't even know how we got to this point. Maybe that's just the process of living with someone for nearly seventeen years. Was it that I just woke up one day and realized that I couldn't stand this woman, that her beauty had just become immaterial? I had begun to question if I had ever really loved her. Travis was the only reason I had chosen to settle down. If she hadn't been pregnant, I would have still been floating around, enjoying my bachelorhood. If I had known that doing "the right thing" would be so damn stressful, I might have just dealt with things from a distance—but I am so thankful for Travis and wouldn't trade in each day I have had with him for anything in the world. I don't think any father could have asked for more in a son. He is my gift from God, my prize for all of the trouble this woman has given me. He is the reason I stick it out and make it work with Bettina.

To place the proverbial nail in the coffin, I say, "Well, maybe it is bullshit. You don't seem to care about what I think any more. I mean, you could have given me a heads-up before you chopped off all of your hair, especially when you know that was a big deal to me."

"This is about my hair?" she huffs. "All you care about is how I look?"

Just when I'm gearing up for a comeback, the phone rings. For a moment the entire room goes silent and all I can hear is the phone ringing. The moment feels very funny, very strange. It's the kind of feeling that you never forget.

Bettina reaches over and picks up the cordless phone from the cradle beside the couch. "Hello," she says disguising the anger in her voice. "Yes, this is Mrs. Thompson."

This all feels wrong.

I'm staring at her now. Suddenly all of my anger is replaced by love and concern for her. She stares back at me and her eyes fill with tears immediately. "No!" she screams, collapsing onto the couch. "Not my baby!"

The phone falls from her hand, and all I can do is run to hold her. She squeezes me as if she is going to tear me apart. My body is numb, and I feel as if I can't control it. I hurt so badly that I'm paralyzed. I know something has just happened to my only son.

I SIT ON THE EDGE OF MY BED AND GLANCE AT THE clock on the dresser next to Travis's picture. It is 4 a.m.

I stand to my feet and turn on the lamp next to my bed. I reach for the phone, but quickly put it down. Who am I going to call at this hour? Melody? That situation is still too new to mess up with something like this. I can just see myself saying, "Melody? Yes. I'm calling you because I just had a nightmare about my son, and I needed you to sit up on the phone with me while I get my head straight." We might get there eventually, but we're not there yet.

For a fleeting moment, the thought of calling Bettina crosses my mind. What the hell is going on with me? I quickly come to my senses. Some doors are best left closed.

I hop in the shower and get dressed for work. By 4:45 I am wrapped in a scarf and my wool trench coat, braving the hawk whipping down through the streets. I stop at a bodega on the corner and pick up a cup of hot chocolate and a cinnamon raisin bagel. By the time I reach TMA, the sun is piercing through the grey of dawn. I unlock the door and go sit down at my desk to eat my breakfast.

As I doodle notes on a pad while sipping my now lukewarm hot chocolate, I am startled by a knock at my door. I look up to see Teresa standing in the doorway with a smile on her face.

"Good morning, Mr. Thompson."

"Good morning, Mrs. Baptiste," I say stifling a smile. Since that first morning we met at the door and had coffee, I had actually missed talking to her.

"I saw your light on in here and just wanted to say hello."

I stand up and gesture for her to have a seat on one of the more "adult-size" chairs near my desk. "Why don't you sit down for a minute? I feel like I haven't talked to you in a while."

"Well," she says. "Let me grab a cup of coffee first,

and I can come back through. That is, unless you're up for coffee yourself."

As I walk with her to the faculty lounge, it occurs to me that I really needed the company this morning. She puts on the coffee and sits down. I take the seat perpendicular to hers.

"You look as if you had a long night, Miles."

"Something like that."

She rises to get two Styrofoam cups from the cabinet above the stove. "Well, if you ever need to talk, I'm here."

"Thanks," I say. "Sometimes I just don't sleep well, so I have to stay active." I don't even know why I'm telling her any of this, but as she hands me a cup of steaming java I feel a connection with this woman.

She takes a seat next to me. "So do you have any plans for this Friday night?"

"Are you asking me out?" I say, half joking.

She laughs and continues, "This organization that Jean-Claude works with is throwing a Halloween masquerade ball this Friday. You're welcome to come through, and you can even bring your friend."

"My friend?"

"Yeah," she says. "The sexy little mami from the play."

She's trying to sound playful, but I can sense a very slight hint of something else in the mix.

"Well, I'll see what 'the sexy little mami' is doing this Friday."

She smiles, "Well, if you could make it, that would be nice."

I take a sip, considering the possibility. "Yeah, we just might drop through."

AT FOUR-THIRTY IN THE AFTERNOON MY CELL phone rings, and Melody's soothing voice oozes through my Bluetooth earpiece. I just finished my last private lesson, and I've been looking forward to hearing her voice all day. Throughout the day I have had mental flashes of her, and while I kind of enjoy Teresa's harmless flirting, I find myself really longing to be with Melody, craving the taste of her lips and the touch of her hands rubbing against my body.

After the initial pleasantries, her first question comes. "Has that boy from the music store come by the school today?"

It takes me a moment to figure out who she's referring to, especially since I've been around a lot of students today. Then I remember Ja Kendrick Brown, the fifteen-year-old music dynamo. "No, I haven't heard from him yet."

"He was really something, wasn't he, Miles?"

"Actually, he was pretty incredible."

"I hope that you two can connect. I think that would be a good thing," she says.

"Well, he'll have to contact *me* since he has my information and I don't have his." OK, enough with the kid, I'm thinking. I'm itching to tell her about the masquerade ball Teresa has invited us to attend and whether or not we're going to see each other tonight. In other words, the things that are primarily on my mind involve her. I move to change the subject. "How was your day?"

"Nothing special. I figure it'll get better as the evening progresses."

"Anything special planned?" I ask.

"That depends on whether or not you'll be available this evening or not," she says sweetly.

"Sure. I'd love to get up with you. What time do you get off?"

"In another hour or so. I just have to wrap up a few things before I leave."

As we start to discuss what time we'll get together, I hear a knock at my door and look up. I don't know why I'm expecting to see Teresa standing there, but to my surprise, a lanky dreadlocked kid with a keyboard swaggers into my classroom.

"Speaking of the devil, " I say into my cell phone. "Let me call you back in a few. I believe Mr. Ja Kendrick Brown has decided to take me up on my offer."

1 2

OCTOBER 25, 2004

JA KENDRICK BROWN

The Thelonius Monk Academy ain't that far from my crib. I didn't have any trouble finding it. What's funny is that I didn't even know that there was anything like it in that neighborhood. The City is like that though: you don't ever know what's around these corners. People coming and going all the time.

I shot the shit with Yusef and Quent for about an hour this afternoon before I bounced and headed up this way. I wanted to make sure I got up with Miles Thompson as soon as possible, but I also didn't really want to fuck with Quent today. When I asked that fool about yesterday, he didn't even deny it. Yeah, that was him, he said. He said he had tried to call Yusef and me but couldn't get up with us. I guess, in theory, that would have been the time that Yusef went to his grandma's crib and the time I was up in Sam Ash. He said that Terrell Bonds had just wanted to introduce him to a few people that Yusef and I could meet later. I don't know. That shit just seems shady to me, but I didn't beef with him about it today. I figured we could just cut it short so I could tend to some other things before five o'clock.

91

Walking down the halls, I can see that the school is a pretty decent size, especially if all you have here is black folks. I pass by five or six classrooms with baby grands in them. By the time I get to the room the woman out front told me was Miles Thompson's, I'm not sure what in the hell to expect. I knock on the opened door and walk in.

Miles is just getting off of his cell phone and stands to shake my hand.

"How's it going, Ja Kendrick?" he says.

"You know, sir. Same stuff, different day." Something about this man just commands my respect, and although I'd hate to admit it, I just want to earn his. I don't want him to think I'm just some other nigga off the block.

"Just call me Miles," he says. "Have a seat at the piano."

I lean Angela up against the wall and walk around and sit down.

"Is that your keyboard? The one you played on the train?" he asks.

"Yes," I respond. "My mother got it for me a long time ago."

"Well, Ja Kendrick, you can do some pretty incredible things with it."

"You can call me Ja," I say, hoping to keep everything easy and smooth. "Thanks though."

"Ja? Interesting," Miles says. "Why not Kendrick?"

"Well, my mama and sister were the only ones to ever call me Kendrick, and my mama's dead."

"Oh, I'm sorry to hear about that."

"It's a'ight. She died back when I was nine."

He looks directly at me, and I feel like a deer in headlights. "I know that had to have been really hard on you."

"You know, it was what it was," I say.

He nods. "What about your sister?"

"Oh, she's never really around, you know. Boyfriend and all." I just can't bring myself to tell him the real deal about how my sister is a junkie with a dough boy boyfriend who almost killed me twice. I don't want to put that shit on him and have him afraid to fuck with me on this music thing.

"Your father?" Miles asks.

"Never knew him."

"Oh," he says. He pauses for a moment and then changes the subject. "Well, I moved here from Atlanta."

"From the Dirty," I say smiling, relieved that we're not talking about my family anymore.

He laughs. "I guess that's what you youngsters would say."

Miles lifts the top lid on the baby grand and places the stand up so that it catches. "Have at it," he says, copping a lean on the edge of his desk.

When my fingers hit the keys, I feel myself letting go. For a moment all I hear is music. I glance down at my hands, and they're moving up and down the board furiously. I don't have any idea of what I'm playing. I'm just letting my fingers slide back and forth across the keys, attempting to keep up with the speed of my thoughts.

"You like chording with your left hand, I see," he says.

"Yeah."

"Are you right handed?"

"Uh, yes," I respond, hands still in motion.

"Tell me again how long have you been playing?"

"Since I was six."

"I can tell that you've been playing for a while because your left hand is really strong. Normally people who haven't been studying that long favor chording with the right hand and just playing off octaves with the left."

"Well, sir. Miles, I mean. I find that I can play more of the music in my head if I can hint at the bass line rather than play it."

He nods. "Interesting."

I continue playing until he stops me.

"Do you read music at the same level you play?" he asks.

"Pretty much."

He reaches over in one of the drawers in his desk and pulls out a book of sheet music, propping it up in front of me. It's a piece by a dude named Sergei Rachmaninoff, and it looks gangsta as hell. I guess he must be trying to peep my skills, because this is hardly some shit you'd expect a person to play for fun or even sight-read.

"Have you ever heard of this piece?" he asks.

I shake my head. I'm still studying the page. There's all kinds of stuff going on in this section, and I can tell by looking at the staff that mood means everything with this piece. I'll be the first to tell you that I don't know everything, but I do know this: Rachmaninoff is a motherfucker.

Miles doesn't say anything, just waits. I feel like I'm under a microscope being scrutinized, but that's a'ight. See, what he don't know is that some of the stuff I wrote ain't that far off this one.

I put my hands on the keys and start to play. Granted, the piece should go a little faster than I'm playing it, I'm still playing through it with no mistakes, as far as I can tell. Out the corner of my eye I can see Miles smiling.

"Not bad, Ja," he says. "Actually, it's pretty damn good."

I try to not to smile too hard. Mama would have

been proud of me if she knew the Miles Thompson thought her son had skillz.

"HEY, MILES," I SAY. "I REALLY APPRECIATE YOU letting me come up through here and play for a minute." We're standing outside in front of Thelonius Monk and the sun's going down.

"No problem. Feel free to come through whenever you want. I'm usually free after four o'clock."

I lift Angela and slide my arm through the large strap on the case. As I turn to walk away, Miles calls after me.

"Yes?" I respond, turning back around.

"Ja, what do you want to do with your gift? You've been blessed with a talent that could take you places."

I put Angela down on the sidewalk next to my feet. "I don't know. I guess I'ma try to get a record deal with my friends. We've already been approached by Big Business Records," I say. "That's a hip hop label."

"That sounds great!" Miles says smiling. "And Ja, I may be older than you, but I do know about Big Business Records. You of all people should know that Big Boze sampled one of my songs."

I can't help but laugh. I forgot Miles had already been in the music business for a minute. Here I am trying to talk to him like he don't know what's up. "That's right," I admit. "But if we can get that deal to go through, we'd be set."

"Well, son," he says. "If you ever need to talk about any of this stuff, you can always come to me. I've been down that road before, and trust me, everything that glitters ain't gold."

"Yes, sir," I say. I wanna ask him what he means, but I don't want to show him how green I am about the music business. Plus, he said I could always come to him with questions, so I'll just wait.

"You be safe getting home," he says, as he locks the front door to the school.

"Thanks," I say. But I'm not really worried about getting home safely. I'm only worried about being safe at home.

As I step off the train, I'm hoping that Daryl is still gone. I sneaked in this morning before school to grab Angela and change clothes, and he had already cut out. I just want to sleep on something soft tonight. When you been sleeping on the train, a couch is like a luxury king-size bed.

The green Hummer is gone, so I'm good. I make my way up the stairs and unlock the door. My sister is sitting on the couch in the den watching TV.

"Sherita, girl, what's up?" I say putting down my backpack and keyboard. I walk over and sit down on the couch beside her. She ignores me, so I tap her on the leg. "'Sup, sis?"

Her voice is a raspy whisper, but I can tell she's not exactly high. "Why do you always have to start shit with Daryl? You know he's the one footing the bills around here."

No "hello, li'l brother." No "where you been 'cause I was worried about you."

I stare at her like she's got a tree growing out the side of her face. I recognize this woman, but I swear I have no idea of what the hell happened to her brain. "He threatened me. I didn't do shit but try to stand up for you!"

"He ain't gonna do nothing to me. He loves me."

"He's all about them c-notes, Sherita. And I don't

care if that nigga is footing the bill. We on rent control anyway. If you would get a job, then we wouldn't need him."

"Me get a job? You get a job, you little motherfucker!"

"It's already enough I stock the fridge with food and buy my own clothes and stuff. And I'm only fifteen! You can't expect me to get a real job."

"I don't give a shit. I got a good thing going with Daryl, and I ain't about to fuck with that. I'm the grown-up in this apartment, and what I say goes."

I lower my head. I swear my sister frustrates the shit out of me.

We sit in silence for a moment, and then I ask a question that I know she doesn't know the answer to: "Is Daryl coming back tonight?"

"Yeah," she says matter-of-factly, but I know she's only hoping.

"Well, I'm gonna take a nap for a little while." I lean my head on the corner of the couch so I can relax.

I'm still mad at her, but I know she's right. I do need to get a job. This record deal has to go through so I can get us out of here.

I pass out with my Tims still strapped to my feet.

13

OCTOBER 25-27, 2004

MILES THOMPSON

"This is absolutely delicious, " I say, as I take a bite of the well-seasoned fish surrounded by rice pilaf and crisp, steamed broccoli. Melody told me the name of the fish, but I can't remember it. All I know is that it's on the more expensive end.

"I'm glad you like it."

We are sitting in the living room of Melody's apartment, and I am totally absorbed in the ambience that she's created with flowers and candles. I can tell that she didn't waste any time when she got home from work. I'm actually flattered that she wanted to start off the week with such a romantic gesture.

She pokes her fork in the spinach and romaine salad on her plate. "How was the rest of your day? How did it go with Ja Kendrick?"

I smile as I think about our meeting. I could tell that Ja Kendrick's playing had impressed Melody as much as it had me. As I escorted her back to her apartment this past Sunday, that was all she could talk about.

"I was pretty surprised when he came through. We talked a little bit about his family. Apparently he lives with his older sister, but I get the impression that he doesn't see her a lot, like he's been pretty much raising himself."

"That's really sad," Melody says. "He's just so gifted!"

"Melody, the kid is incredible." I take a sip from the glass of white wine at the edge of my plate. "He played for me today and blew me away!"

"That's so wonderful!" she says, smiling. "I told you that you two would hit it off."

"And he reads music at an extremely high level. I wouldn't be surprised if Ja Kendrick played better than a number of those students over at Julliard."

"So what does he want to do with his talent?"

"He says he's working on a record deal with a few of his friends."

Melody's eyes dance as she puts her glass down. "Are you serious?"

"Oh yes."

"How cool is that? Maybe you could help him out with some of that stuff."

"Well, if he asks me, I will."

We finish up our dinner, and I follow her into the bedroom.

Soft, sweet music drifts through the bedroom speakers, and we make love by candlelight, our bodies floating in a buzzing haze of liquor and lust. I feel the weight of my thoughts give way to her warm caresses as I dissolve into her, and for the first time in a long time, I feel myself letting go.

"WAKE UP, BABY!" IS THE FIRST THING I HEAR. Melody's usual musical tone has a sense of urgency in it. "Every time I wake you, you keep going right back to sleep!"

My eyes open to Melody's beautiful golden face. Her hair has been done, and her makeup is in place. In fact, as I ease up on my elbows, I notice that not only is she completely dressed for work, but the sun is also blazing down through the blinds into her bedroom.

"What time is it?" I ask, still confused. For the last few weeks I had been waking up at four in the morning, so I am still in shock.

"It's seven. You might have to get a cab back to your apartment if you're going to make it to work on time."

"Oh, shit!" I yell, hopping out of the bed. I begin dressing as quickly as my hands will move.

"Call me later," Melody says, as I kiss her and dart out the apartment.

SITTING AT MY DESK AFTER ARRIVING AT MY classroom a few minutes late, I am still confused. I guess I had taken for granted that I couldn't oversleep. Once you've had a nightmare for so long, you get used to dealing with it. Last night I must not have had one. Instead of being relieved that I didn't have one, I'm scratching my head wondering what happened to change that.

After giving out a writing assignment to my restless class, I sit down at my desk and try to figure this whole thing out. Naturally, my mind goes to the incredible evening I had with Melody last night. I think of her sweet lips kissing down my chest, her fingers interlocked with mine as she grinds her hips into my mine. I think about the softness of those athletic legs wrapping around my waist. I think about her breasts cupped in my hands, my tongue flickering at her nipples. I think about her soft voice, punctuated by exclamations of ecstasy. I even think about the feeling of our bodies colliding in a fury of orgasmic energy. It had been amazing, I admit to myself. That must be it then. Melody wore me out last night. Why is that so surprising?

I'm almost convinced of my theory until I have more time to explore it during the lunch period. Sitting at my desk, I realize that Saturday and Sunday nights with Melody had been nothing short of amazing either. The problem was that I had had nightmares on both nights. Saturday evening I played it off by easing out of bed to watch infomercials on the television in her den. On Sunday night, I came back to my apartment, particularly because I didn't want to run the risk of being late for work yesterday. The nightmares had come like clockwork. What was so different about last night then?

I replayed the entire day in my head. Could it have been Teresa? I seriously doubt it. The only other thing unique about Monday was my meeting with Ja Kendrick. Meeting up with a fifteen year old to discuss music doesn't really strike me as the kind of thing that could do away with several weeks of nightmares. Maybe it was Melody after all. Or maybe I just slept through the nightmare this time.

I really should just leave it alone and count my blessings. Getting a real peaceful night's sleep is a rarity I should embrace, not question.

I STAYED AT THE SCHOOL UNTIL 5:30 P.M., UNSURE of whether or not Ja Kendrick would show up. He didn't. Melody called to tell me that she had to stay late at the office to work on a project because some major clients from Boston were coming down on Friday. She did agree to come with me to the Halloween masquerade, though.

Left with an open evening, I caught the 3 train down to Brooklyn Heights to enjoy a scoop of ice cream on the promenade while gazing at the skyline of Manhattan. I used to do this a lot during that first summer when I moved here, but since then, I've allowed myself to get wrapped up in everything else and come up with every excuse in the world to not make the trek down here.

Sitting here now, as the sun sets beyond the East River, the image of the parallel lights beaming up from where the Twin Towers used to stand sends a haunting chill up my spine. For a moment it makes me think of my own loss. But life keeps on moving right along, I tell myself, although I have come to find that sometimes it's a chore just to keep up with it.

Buildings stand out boldly in the auburn haze of lights that hang like a fog over the water.

I take a slow lick from the top scoop of my butter pecan, careful not to knock it from the thin sugar cone. A cool breeze whips up behind me, reminding me that my choice of a snack might have been a little ill-considered, but I've always had a thing for ice cream. In the early years of my marriage, Bettina would often mess with me about my craving for ice cream in the depths of winter. It all seems like another life now.

Resting on the bench, I notice couples walking in warming embraces, and I even see a few people out walking their dogs. It seems as if everyone has found his or her own niche in the City, so maybe it's time that I turn myself over to this new life that I've created. I mean, I have a job that is satisfying on so many different levels, I have a woman who is beautiful and smart and actually gives a damn about me, and I have a city full of just about everything that I could ever want. I'm beginning to think that that was the point of my not having a nightmare last night: just to show me that it's officially time to move on with life, to stop beating myself up over Bettina and Travis.

As the thought settles over me, I find a kind of peace seeping through the cracks in my tense mind. I look over to my left, and I can scarcely make out the outline of the Statue of Liberty through the hazy glow of the well-lit skyline. With the taste of butter pecan still dancing on my taste buds, I imagine that freedom from the pain of my past is even sweeter.

I AM STRETCHED OUT ON THE RECLINER IN THE DEN OF my old house in Atlanta, an issue of Black Enterprise *draped across my lap. Other than the soft sound of white noise from the TV in the background, the room is quiet.*

I begin to hum a melody, a simple melody that loops over and over—but then I hear it! It sounds like a piano somewhere in the distance, hiding behind the sound of my own voice. I rise slowly, looking around for some indication that the sound is coming from the television or the stereo speakers in the corners of the room.

I stand beneath one of the speakers, straining to hear. The melody continues, but after placing my hand against the speaker, I realize the sound is not coming from this room. It sounds like it's coming from the hall, so I begin walking toward it. As I enter the hall, the piano melody grows louder. Standing at the base of the stairs leading up to the bedrooms, I can hear the sound more clearly. A piano is playing the melody that I had just been humming.

I slowly walk up the stairs. I don't remember there being so many of them, but it seems as if I am climbing and climbing, with the top of the stairs laughing at my futile attempt to ascend them. My steps become more labored, as if I am slowly walking up an escalator moving in the opposite direction.

Eventually I reach the top of the stairs. The master bedroom is at the end of the hall on the left. Travis's room is in the middle of the hall on the right. By now the music is loud, and what was once a simple melody has become a chorded complexity that scarcely resembles the original. I look at Travis's door, and it is almost completely closed, save a small crack beckoning me forward.

"Travis?" I call out through a mask of confusion. I repeat his name again.

There is no response.

I approach the door, feeling as if I'm being lured by the music. For a flashing moment, I think of the masses of children following the Pied Piper to an unknown fate. I stretch out my hand and push the door open. The room is three times larger than I ever remember it being. In the heart of the room is a large black grand piano with the lid elevated to release an explosion of sound. As I adjust to the sight of the piano, the music seamlessly morphs into Beethoven's posthumously titled "Moonlight Sonata." My son is playing the piano!

I can't see his face beyond the looming darkness of the piano, so I edge closer, still amazed that Travis has actually learned to play his father's instrument of choice. I walk slowly around the side of the piano, my hand tracing the black polished wood. The haunting sound of Beethoven circles through the air like a stream of incense smoke.

"Travis, that's absolutely beautiful," I say, stepping around the piano.

With a shadow looming over him, bathing him in darkness, I see a young man, roughly my son's age, with his head lowered allowing his dreadlocks to fall like a silk sheet across his face. His shoulders are rising and falling *with the rolling of his fingers across the keys. His head sways rhythmically back and forth, and it makes me think of a curtain rustling in the wind. This is not my son.*

This is the young man who has transformed my dreams.

14

OCTOBER 28, 2004

JA KENDRICK BROWN

Sometimes when I'm chilling in class, I wonder about the future. Mama always said I needed to do my best in school to give myself some options for later on. Truth be told, the only reason I do a'ight in school now is because I got this photographic memory. I just read shit and remember it. If it wasn't for my teachers making a big deal of "remembering" things for tests, I would've probably flunked out a long time ago. That memory has kept me at a "B" average.

I'm a sophomore at Martin Luther King, Jr. High School, just biding my time 'til I graduate. My school is in a pretty rough neighborhood, but I grew up with most of the knuckleheads there, so I don't have any real enemies. Also, I don't really spend a lot of time hanging out there when classes let out. I'm just trying to be about mines and make something happen with this music thing.

School is bullshit though. Most of the teachers don't wanna be there. They think that teaching in the 'hood is some kind of paid community service project or something. And while we got some wild boys up in here, we ain't really a bad group. We definitely ain't like the kids in the Bronx who suck dick in the halls between classes and cuss their teachers out, but it don't matter; we get treated the same way they do. I really wanted to try out for a performing arts school like La-Guardia, but my sister was going through some shit around the time they had auditions, and I wasn't too cool with the idea of traveling way across town just to go to school, music or no music. Plus, I don't need some old dude grading me on something I know like the back of my hand. What kind of sense does that make?

I guess that's why I haven't been back to see Miles Thompson. Like I said, I respect him, but I can't really figure out his angle. I mean, what does a dude on his level want with a Harlem kid like me. I can play a little bit, yeah, but I know he has to know a lot of cats who can get down on the keys. Why single me out though? I hope he ain't funny. Nah, he ain't funny. He ain't got that kinda vibe.

I guess I'm just buggin' out 'cause good shit don't normally happen to me. I've just been fucked over enough times in my life to always wait for the other boot to drop.

I should probably get up with Miles sometime soon, though. He *could* be the real deal, and it would be stupid of me to just blow that because I got caught up in some rah-rah shit in my head.

THIS TIME WE AGREED TO MEET UP AT THE STUDIO.

Approaching the building, I notice Yusef standing out in front beside the door.

"What's up, Ja?" he says, gripping me.

"Samo samo," I respond.

"Quent ain't made it here yet."

I wanna rap with Yusef about Quent and all of this

undercover shit, but I'm not really sure of how he'll take it. Maybe I'm just paranoid, and I don't want him looking at me sideways. "What do you think about all of this?" I ask, just to smoke him out.

"You know, I been thinking 'bout this a little, and I'm trying to figure out all the angles."

"You too?" I say, relieved that I'm not the only one feeling funny.

"Yeah. It all sounds good, but I can't really tell where everyone is coming from. The worst part is I can't really tell what side of the fence Quent is on," Yusef says. "I'm thinking that he must have been up with these niggas for a while before he put us in the loop."

I nod. "You think he was scoping a solo deal and Terrell told him a group might fly better?"

"If you had asked me that same question last year I would've said hell no. Now I'm thinking anything is possible with you put a dollar in the mix."

I'm always impressed at how Yusef breaks things down. I've been told that I got street smarts, but Yusef is on a whole other level. It's like a sixth sense with him. He can always tell if a person is happy, sad, high, horny, crazy, sneaky, or full of shit in just a glance.

"I hope this is the real thing though," I say. "I could use the ends, for real."

"Can't we all."

I look down toward 42nd and 8th and see Quent coming up the block.

"Yo, son!" he says, dapping me and then Yusef.

"I guess we should head on up to see what's going on," Yusef says, as he holds the door open for us.

When we step off the elevator, my gut gets tight. I feel like I need to take one of those "nervous shits" to clear my stomach. Before I even have a chance to get my mind right, I see her: jeans clingin' to those sexy ass legs, sweater tight across her breasts with just a sliver of her stomach showing so you can peep the belly ring. Lei Morgan, the kind of woman a brotha could marry.

I approach her like a long lost friend. "Lei!"

She looks at me and smiles. I'm surprised when she reaches out and hugs me.

"I was beginning to wonder if I'd ever run into you again," she says. "Smoke-T has been talking non-stop about you guys for the past week or so."

I try to keep from cheesing, but the thought of her actually checking for me since the last time I saw her makes a brotha feel like he's on some Denzel shit. "Well, you know, we just been hustlin' and keeping busy."

Quent signals from down the hall that we need to go straight to the office. I turn back to Lei. "So can I get your number so we don't have to wonder if we'll ever cross paths again?"

"Sure."

She gives me her number, and I jot it down on a piece of paper. I'm embarrassed by the fact that I don't have a cell phone yet. When I get my ends straight, I'll make that the first thing I get.

"If you're still around when we get done in the office, maybe we could talk a little bit," I say.

"Well, the girls and I are headed to a photo shoot, but just give me a call when you get a minute."

"Most definitely," I say, hugging her again and heading off down the hall.

<hr>

As soon as we get through rehearsing our audition song, Terrell Bonds comes through the door with a tall, dark-skinned brother rocking this black pinstripe suit and red power tie. The guy's suit looks like it cost a fortune, and he looks even richer than Terrell, which I didn't really think was possible.

"Whassup, guys?" Terrell says. "This is Teddy Ray, the head honcho over at Big Business. We just want you guys to do that song you did for us the other day."

As we gear up and let loose on the Triumph's song again, a warm feeling comes over me. I see Teddy's head nodding to the rhythm of the music and the singing. Terrell is smiling and nodding to the beat, too. It feels good when we finally finish the song, like someone lifted a giant boulder off my shoulders.

"You kids are great!" Teddy says. "I'm gonna to sit down with Terrell and see what we can do to get this project off the ground."

Quent, Yusef, and I are so excited we're bouncing off the walls like we hit for the Powerball, dapping each other like crazy. This is what we've been working for all this time. Big Business Records! Who woulda thought?

When we step out the building to go our separate ways, I look up at the skyscrapers all around me and feel like I can touch the top of each of them.

15

OCTOBER 28, 2004

MILES THOMPSON

Ja Kendrick is still a no-show, so I head over to the train station so I can get to the costume store in the East Village before they close. When I finally manage to get a seat on the bustling train, I end up seated between an Asian-American guy with a folded paper hat on his head and a thirty-something Latino brother with his two-year-old daughter seated on his lap.

"What color is Winnie the Pooh?" the father asks his daughter, loud enough for everyone to hear.

"Yellow," the little girl responds in a tiny voice.

I look over at her cute little face and the dancing innocence in her eyes as she awaits her father's next question. I smile at her and return to reading the ads above the doors and windows on the train. "Learn Spanish," one says. Another asks if I have been a victim of the drug Vioxx. Another is an inventive short poem being used to advertise for a bookstore chain.

"What color is a fire truck?" the father continues.

"Red."

"What color is Tigger?"

The girl struggles to form the word "orange" in her mouth. For a moment I think about Travis at her age.

He was a smart kid, too. I wonder if Ja Kendrick was like that growing up. It wouldn't surprise me if he were.

I exit the train at Union Square and head over to the store. Instinctively, I reach for my cell phone to call Melody.

"Miles," she answers in her sultry voice. "How are you doing, baby?"

"I'm good," I say, imagining her body the night before last. "I'm down here in the Village about to pick up a costume for the masquerade ball tomorrow. I wanted to know if you wanted me to pick you up anything to wear."

"What did you have in mind?"

"Well, I was thinking that I could go as John Shaft, and you could go as Foxy Brown."

Melody laughs. "Miles, I would have thought that as an artist you wouldn't be so cliché!"

"Oh, so you got jokes?" I say laughing. To be honest, I didn't really have any idea of what I was supposed to be looking for in the first place. "What about Dracula and Elvira?"

"I've gone to Halloween parties as Elvira so many times that I had to officially retire the costume a few years ago."

"Ike and Tina? Hey, I'm running out of ideas."

I can hear her laughing through the phone. "Why don't you look for an Egyptian King and Queen costume set or some other type of royalty costumes?"

Actually her suggestion is a pretty good idea. "That could work," I say.

"Well, if you want, you could come by for dinner tonight and show me what you picked out."

"Sounds good. I'll see you then."

As I walk around the maze of horror costumes, celebrity masks, and large plastic bags full of cheap fabric, I scan the store for anything that looks like an Egyptian get-up. Behind a few rows of colonial style clothing, I see the headpiece for an Egyptian king costume and the accompanying neck/chest ornamental dressing and a white robe with a gold trim. Next to it is the complete outfit for the queen. Looking at the flowing white fabric trimmed in gold, I imagine the costume clinging to Melody's petite figure, and I smile. After the party, maybe we could use these costumes for a little role-playing.

I reach for the price tag, shaking my head as I take in the figure. No wonder these people stay in business, I think to myself. As I glance around the store and then at my watch, I decide to grab the costumes so that I can still make it by Melody's place fairly early. I won't be staying with her tonight because she has to get up early for a presentation at work tomorrow.

Then the thought hits me that I've been seeing a lot of this woman. Classically, I've never been one for committed relationships, and although we haven't had that discussion yet, it is starting to feel pretty exclusive. Part of me welcomes a relationship with her; the other part of me, the part that existed before and after Bettina, is not anxious to make that level of commitment right now. My friend Richard Hardiman used to say, "Don't worry about making decisions on love. Your heart will let you know what to do when the time is right." I don't know if I ever bought that, especially from a man who married his high school sweetheart, but it's as good a suggestion as any.

———

I HAVEN'T BEEN OUT OF THE STORE FOR TWO minutes before I start to question my having dropped more than three hundred dollars on some faux

Egyptian costumes that will probably only get worn once or twice at best. Buyer's remorse is what they call it, and I almost step back inside to do an exchange for something else. The only problem is that costumes are to Halloween as roses are to Valentine's Day, so it would be difficult to come out too much cheaper. I quickly visualize Melody dressed as an Egyptian queen, her body moving rhythmically as she walks into the room. I see her dimpled smile spreading across her honey-tinted lips. I see her long curly hair dancing atop her shoulders. I even feel her soft, full lips pressed against mine as her hands caress the small of my back and her body falls weightlessly into mine.

I tuck the bag under my arm and continue toward the train. I guess in the end I don't have a problem being a king, and as funny as it is for me to admit this, I don't really have a problem with Melody being my queen either.

16

OCTOBER 28, 2004

MELODY LITHCOTT

I have always believed that everything happens for a reason. I know that there must be some major force at work allowing things to unfold as they do.

Fifteen years ago, I left my job as an executive administrative assistant to marry a man I thought was the most amazing person on the planet.

I met Howard Donaldson at the annual Christmas party hosted by the local Black professionals organization a year earlier. I had only gone that night because my best friend, Gina Lassiter, and her husband, Frank, invited me to come out of my antisocial shell and enjoy myself among some of the more "upwardly mobile African Americans" in Charlotte, North Carolina.

The area of the convention center that had been sectioned off for the party was beautifully decorated with lights, cotton snow, forest green wreaths wrapped in brilliant red bows, and a fifteen foot Christmas tree trimmed in extravagant gold and red ornaments, complete with empty gift wrapped boxes circling beneath.

Not being a fan of overly bourgeois people, I stayed close to Gina and Frank, fearful of being locked in a conversation with one of those men who feels he is

God's gift to women simply because he has a six-figure salary and a German-made convertible sitting in front of his condo. I had dated a man for money once, and it was one of the worst experiences of my life. He was so into himself, and all he ever cared about was what he was going to buy with his money next. Not only was he horrible in the bed (he was hung like a light switch, but swore he was Mandingo), he was just soft all the way around. I honestly don't like to date men who think they are more beautiful than women; that just seems so backward to me. Even the little trinkets he gave me didn't quell the emptiness I got from being around him. I vowed to never use a brother's bank account as a priority in deciding whom I should date. As long as he had a job, was fun to be around, preferably attractive, and wanted to do something with his life, I would be fine.

The night I met Howard, he had managed to ease up next to me and "accidentally" bump into me as I sipped on a glass of wine. I almost spilled the wine all over my cream pantsuit. Just as I turned in his direction, prepared to unleash my wrath over his clumsiness, I met his eyes and started to melt. He was over six feet tall, a deep chocolate complexion, his hair shaved off completely with a razor, and with the exception of his strong eyebrows and long eyelashes, his face was hairless. He looked like a Milk Dud with eyes, but in a good way.

He quickly apologized, and that apology turned into a conversation that led to a date. A year later we married at that same convention center. Gina served as my matron-of-honor.

During our honeymoon, Howard informed me that he didn't want me to be "anybody's secretary" and pushed me to quit my job, while he supported both of us from his salary as a dermatologist. Five years later, we moved into a quaint house in Secaucus, New Jersey, so that he could start up a new private practice with one of his classmates from Cornell University Medical College. I didn't mind at all, and the lure of New York City nearby was more than an attractive notion.

And for a while everything was great.

Then one day during the seventh year of our marriage I found a condom in the back pocket of one of his pants. It seemed almost comical at first, like a scene out of some melodramatic soap opera, but there it was. Real. And this was my life, not some television show. I didn't do anything crazy though. I just spent the rest of the afternoon combing through the rest of the house looking for anything that could help to confirm what I was starting to believe.

I went through every closet, every drawer, every file on the computer in our office, every nook and cranny I could fit my fingers between, and by the end of the day I had discovered a box of condoms (none of which we had ever used), a 4x6 picture of an over-tanned white woman with bleached blonde hair, and the coup de grat: digitals pictures of Howard receiving a blow job from the same blonde woman and other pictures of him penetrating her from various positions, all hidden within ten layers of file folders under obscure names on the hard drive of our computer.

After I managed to pick myself up from the floor and wipe the storm of tears that had come down on me like a hurricane, I felt like a fool. He must have truly thought I was stupid if he could hide so much stuff around me without me finding out. Or maybe he did want me to find them because he was too weak and pathetic to tell me himself. How could all of this have been going on under my nose the entire time? I didn't have a job, so my entire existence was maintaining the house and trying to keep that Negro happy. Now I didn't have anything, and that thought scared the hell out of me.

I immediately called Gina and cried on the phone to her for several hours. By the time I got off the phone, she had agreed to fly up from Charlotte and stay with me for a few days.

That last night with Howard was the hardest thing in the world. I pretended to act as if everything was normal, ignoring his desire to make love before bed. The following morning when he left for work, I went to pick up Gina from the airport, and we immediately took the steps to getting the locks changed on the doors. Then we called around and found a lawyer who didn't mind giving Howard "da business" or as my favorite boxer Mike Tyson once put it so eloquently, "stomp on his testicles." Howard had fucked me, but I wasn't going to let him get away with it. I was determined to fuck him back.

Of course, in retrospect, I am probably looking at my former self as being much stronger than I really was when I went through all of that bullshit. The reality is probably more like this: I was in a state of emotional paralysis half the time, and Gina helped to guide me through a lot of the decisions I had to make that would eventually allow me get the house, the 500 series Benz, a hefty alimony, and my maiden name back.

I eventually got a job as an assistant at an event-planning agency, but everything was very slow and painful for a while. I did my best to learn as much as I could at work, gradually gaining more responsibility, but when I would go home at night, I felt as if I were trapped in an empty castle, a queen without a king. Every corner of the house held some kind of memory of my marriage, and I had to get a prescription just to go to sleep at night.

Then one day I got a call from Gina saying that she

and Frank were moving to Brooklyn so that he could accept an associate professor position at Brooklyn College. I felt as if a prayer had been answered!

When Gina and Frank finally arrived, everything began to look up for me. I had close friends around me who actually cared about me and wanted to be there for me while I got through the transition of being recently divorced. I even started working out at the gym again to take off the thirty or so pounds I had picked up since I had gotten married. With the two of them supporting me, I eventually lowered my guard enough to go on the occasional date. But more than anything, I used that time to get to know who I really was and what it was that I felt I truly wanted and deserved out of life.

MILES THOMPSON IS A TOTALLY UNEXPECTED addition to my life. I never thought that I would feel so strongly about another man as I do now. It took so much to get me to a point where I could even make myself available to the possibility of being involved with someone on the level that Miles and I are. And it's really wonderful!

When Gina first told me that Frank had mentioned me to Miles at the gym one day, I was really embarrassed. I didn't want to come across as some desperate woman. And when Gina told me that Miles was the same Miles Thompson from The Triumphs, I became even more embarrassed. Now I would look like some kind of groupie.

I debated what I would do if he should call me. I hadn't been on a blind date since I was a teenager, and the idea of going on one in my forties just didn't sound so appealing.

I dug up my old albums and listened to The Triumphs' songs while pouring over the various pictures of the group. Although Miles wasn't the lead singer, he was quite popular—if my memory serves correctly—because he was the most handsome one. Reading the credits to the songs, especially the ones that I had enjoyed the most, I noticed an "M. Thompson" in the parenthesis besides a number of those songs. Suddenly I felt even more nervous about the prospect of his calling. Frank was really trying to mess a sister up by putting me on blast like that.

I had just transferred to the New York office of my agency and sold the house, opting to move into a nice, cozy spot on the Upper West Side. A lot was going on, a lot of changes in my life, and after playing with the idea for what seemed like forever, I decided that if Miles called asking me out, I would accept.

He called early one evening, and we talked for a while. He was charming and sweet, not at all boring or self-absorbed, so I agreed to meet him for a play. I had no idea that we would hit it off like we did!

After agreeing to get together that Saturday at Central Park, I knew that I wanted to really be closer to him. It's like we clicked, and all I wanted to do was be near him, touch him, listen to him, hold him.

And when we had sex, I almost lost my mind. He entered me and filled me up so deeply that I had to catch my breath for a moment. It was like he was hitting my spot and a few other spots that I didn't even know I had. He moved gently back and forth inside of me, caressing my breasts with his strong hands while kissing my lips, cheeks, and forehead with those delicious lips of his. I came so hard that it scared me. He just seemed too perfect. I just wanted to wrap myself in his arms and shield myself from the world.

WE'VE BEEN GOING OUT FOR A WHILE NOW, AND I'm starting to get to a point where I can't imagine being without him. And that's scary. I just don't normally trust that men can be faithful. Maybe Miles is different though. He seems different. He seems like he actually has feelings for me. I can feel it when he holds me late at night or when I hear his voice on the phone or when he enters me. It feels like he's making love to me, not fucking me. As much as I try to tease and flirt with him, keeping the upper hand, I feel myself becoming more and more vulnerable to him.

And I feel him opening up to me more each day too. The other night while he slept, he wrestled in his sleep, as if he was having a nightmare. When I got him to wake up, I massaged his shoulders and asked him what he had dreamed of.

He looked at me as if he was unsure of whether or not he wanted to open that much of himself to me and then said, "I had a nightmare about my son."

While I massaged his shoulders, he spoke softly and tenderly about Travis and the sequence of events that had led him to New York. That same night I told him about Howard and what had happened to me. While the conversation was very heartfelt and open, I thought I might have scared him off or rubbed him the wrong way by giving up so much information on my background so quickly. Interestingly, though, we have spent almost every night together since then.

I am seriously considering just making the first move and asking for an exclusive relationship with him. It's the 21st century, and gender formalities don't matter anymore. I know what I want, and I know that he can give that to me. I want him, and I don't want to share him with anyone. I know that it seems almost

180 degrees from what we talked about that day down in the East Village where I told him that I was cool just dating, but back then, I was still feeling the situation out. It's one thing to think a man is fine and want to fuck him; it's a whole other thing to think a man is wonderful and want to love him.

I think I'll bring up my feelings with him this Friday at the masquerade ball.

17

OCTOBER 29, 2004

JA KENDRICK BROWN

I was still sleeping this morning when Daryl came busting through the apartment door. He dropped his keys on the table like a brick. It was like he was trying to wake me up. I pretended to be asleep while he walked around the apartment. At one point I swear I could feel him standing over me, looking down at me, but I was too scared to open my eyes. If he thought I was even awake, he might've just commenced to kicking my ass right there. After all, this was the first time I'd been here since he pushed me into the wall and threatened to kill me.

After a while, I could hear him stomp into the bedroom in the back and close the door.

I knew I'd be sleeping on the train tonight.

I WAKE UP AND STAND TO STRETCH MY BACK. THE bathroom is empty, so I jump in and shower as fast as I can, brushing my teeth at the same time. When I dry off, I grab a hooded sweatshirt and jeans out the closet in the den.

When I'm dressed, I put Angela in the closet by

the door and head out to MLK High School, the hallowed halls of the 'hood. I can't help but think about how much I miss Mama. If she knew what was going on with Sherita, she would have shut down shop real quick. When Mama was well, she was strong and smart, and she didn't take no shit off no one. I remember one time some guy Mama was going out with made a pass at Sherita. Rather than side with her man like some desperate female, she got in dat ass and kicked ole boy to the curb. I smile when I think about how gangsta Mama used to be.

When she first passed, I was pretty messed up. I couldn't stop crying that first week. After Sherita had finally convinced me to calm down some, I really started getting more into my keyboard. I would study that book Mama gave me and spend hours playing whatever was in it. From time to time Auntie Sarah would buy me new books, each of them joints a little harder than the last.

Back then, Auntie Sarah was living back and forth between her apartment and ours. Then she had that first stroke, and Sherita had to get a job to make ends meet. After Auntie Sarah had a third stroke, coupled with her blood sugar, the doctors had to take both of her legs. For a while she was in a nursing home in Brooklyn where I would visit her from time to time. About six months after Auntie Sarah went in, she passed in her sleep. The craziest thing is that the last thing she told me before she got sick was, "I just wanna die in one piece." In the end she couldn't even get that.

I shake my head to clear my thoughts. If I dwell on all of that stuff, my eyes start to water, and I ain't trying to look soft when I get to school. I run my hand through my back pocket to find the scrap of paper Lei Morgan wrote her number on. It's still there. I'm guessing I should try to call her this afternoon since it's Friday and all. I should probably also swing by and holler at Miles so that he don't think I'm flaking on him. I just have to keep myself busy for the rest of the day since I can't go home.

WHEN I PICK UP THE PHONE THE BUTTERFLIES IN my stomach are flapping so hard that I almost hang up the and say, "Screw this." I think about what Yusef's crazy ass would say about being nervous when it came to a girl. He always says, "If you're gonna talk to a fine sister for the first time and you're nervous, then you gotta take a 'nervous shit' to get the butterflies out your system." I remember laughing at him, but now I'm getting the drift. I could definitely have used at least ten minutes in a bathroom stall somewhere to get right before I picked up the phone to make this call.

The phone rings three times before someone answers.

"Hello?"

"Uh, hello," I manage. "Can I speak to Lei?"

"May I ask who's calling?"

"Uh, yes, this is Ja Kendrick Brown. I know her from the Big Business studio off 42nd Street."

"Oh, you do, Mr. Brown?" the voice says, as if quizzing me.

"Yes. Is she around?"

"Well, that depends, Mr. Brown. Why would you like to speak to her?"

What the hell is going on? I ask myself. All the while my stomach is turning flips and all kind of pressure is churning in my guts.

"I just wanted to say whassup and touch bases with her. You know, see if the number was good," I say.

There is a burst of laughter from the other end, and I hear the phone changing hands. "Hello?" a new voice says.

"Hello," I say again. "May I speak to Lei?"

"Hi, Ja!" she says, laughing. "This is Lei. You'll have to forgive my girl Tasha. She likes messing with people who call me."

"Oh," I say, adding a fake chuckle. "That's cool."

"So what's going on, Ja?" Her voice is so smooth, like she's been waiting for my call.

"Just hustling on the humble. But really I just wanted to get at you before you forgot who I was," I say.

"Yeah, I was just thinking 'what's the name of that cute boy I met at the studio?'" she says with a light laugh. "Like I would have actually forgotten who you were."

I laugh at this, partially because it was funny, partially because I hadn't been hit with a compliment like that in a minute and didn't want to look all corny on my end. "So when can we get up and chat? Face-to-face, you know?"

"You don't waste any time, do you, Ja?" she says.

Thinking about the fact that I'm feeding quarters into a pay phone outside of a bodega in Harlem, I say, "Well, I know your time is precious, so I just wanted to put it out there that I was available, if you were."

"Hmm. They have us on a pretty tight schedule these days, with the album release date coming up in a couple of months."

My stomach drops. I'm really fucking this up. I shouldn't have been so straight forward. I must've scared her.

She continues, "I have a few hours during the day tomorrow. Can you meet up in the morning, say around ten, on the corner of Houston and Broadway? I have to be down there tomorrow for another early morning photo shoot."

"That's cool," I say. There's no point in playing hard to get, especially after I've already shown my hand. "I can do that."

"OK. Good. Well, Ja, I have to run, but I'll see you on the corner of Houston and Broadway tomorrow at ten."

"Sounds great," I say.

I hang up the phone. Across the street I see this dude with his girl, all booed up like they just came out of a Spike Lee flick, and it doesn't take me two seconds to realize that I want something like that, too.

As I walk down the street, I keep thinking about the phone call. I can't help but think of how good it sounded to hear her say my name. And she just kept on saying it, too! Now my stomach is really doing a number!

Focus, I tell myself. This is all you, son. You got this.

"To what do I owe this honor?" Miles says, faking like he's surprised when I walk into his classroom. He's standing next to his desk, getting his stuff together.

"Well, I've been trying to keep up with everything," I say. "I'm sorry I ain't been able to get back over here."

"That's all right. I understand," he responds. "But I'm going to have to cut it pretty short today because I have an event to get to tonight."

I feel kinda stupid now. I just assumed that he'd be here ready to roll whenever I came through. He's obviously a busy man, and he probably has a lot of better stuff to do than sit around waiting on me. "Well, I can walk you to your cab or train or whatever," I offer.

"Sure. I don't live too far from here, so we can actually walk if you have the time."

When I accept, I have no idea of how far we'll be walking, but after about ten blocks, I'm beginning to wonder if we're headed to Brooklyn. Miles is walking this shit with some serious ease, because he's keeping a pretty strong pace.

"So how have you been?" he asks.

"Everything is still looking good with the record deal. We got to perform for Teddy Ray, the CEO of Big Business, a few days ago, and I think he really liked us."

"That's great news. I'm glad to see that things are working out for you."

"What was it like when you and The Triumphs got signed?"

"Oh, man. That was a long time ago. Different cast of characters back then," he says. "We were still in school at Ellison-Wright when a guy named Jay Jackson heard us perform at the homecoming coronation and wanted to sign us. Up to that point, nothing better had ever happened to me in my life."

I feel special when he tells me about how five guys from the South broke into the music game in the late seventies. I keep thinking that there're probably a million other guys out there who would love to be getting the 411 from this dude, and here I am, able to ask whatever I want and get some real knowledge in the process.

"I bet you guys made a ton of money," I say.

"That's the interesting part, Ja. The group itself made decent money, but truth be told, I probably made out a little bit better than a lot of the other guys."

As we finally approach his building—thank God—I ask, "How so?"

"Something that most industry guys don't want the artist to know is that most of the real money comes from songwriting. I didn't write all of the songs for The Triumphs, but the few that I did write went over well. Got a lot of radio airplay, usage on television and in films, and of course the mechanicals, which are royalties the record company pays you for putting your song on the album."

Songwriting? All I can think about is all of the rappers and R&B singers lined up in front of Bentleys with fine ass women standing around putting a buff on the hood with their titties. All because they wrote their own songs though?

"So what you're saying is if this deal goes through, then I need to make sure I write a few songs for the album?"

"That would be ideal."

"What about the guy who sings lead and the other guys in the group?"

"Well, back in the day they used to give the group an advance that was split up among everyone in the group. The good thing is that it put some change in your pocket. The bad thing is that you didn't get any more money on the album until you've made back what they gave you, and you had to make back that money from the small royalty you got off of each album. Literally pennies."

I'm starting to get confused with all of this music business language, so I ask, "Is it OK for me to come by on Monday afternoon and talk with you about all of this? It's kind of heavy stuff, and I might need for you to school me on what to expect when all of this stuff goes down."

"No problem," Miles says, starting up the stairs to

open the front door to the apartment building. "You can come up if you want."

"Naw, man, I'm cool. I know you gotta get ready to go to something, so I'll just get up with you next week," I say. "Have fun tonight, though."

"Sure thing, Ja."

As I turn to walk back toward the train station he calls out after me, "Hey, if you need anything, don't hesitate to call me."

I nod. "A'ight. Thanks."

OCTOBER 29, 2004

MILES THOMPSON

Our cab pulls up in front of a huge red brick building off Lafayette and Prince Street in SoHo, and I lift Melody's hand from my lap, kissing it softly. With the makeup and eyeliner emphasizing the Egyptian queen costume she's wearing, she reminds me of Cleopatra. She smiles as I kiss her hand again, and for a moment I lose myself in her large, beautiful eyes. Just as I venture to kiss her lips, the cab driver clears his throat, clearly wanting to get his fee so he can return to driving other people to their various Halloween events all over the City.

"That'll be $12.80," the cab driver says, through a thick accent.

I hand him a twenty as both Melody and I exit the cab. Before I can ask for change, the cab is zooming down Prince Street like a thief in the night. Melody doesn't notice my displeasure with the cab driver, so I put on a calm face as I escort her up the stairs of the building.

Walking over to the elevators beyond the empty security desk, I catch a reflection of both of us in the mirror, our trench coats covering our costumes.

"You know, we make a nice looking couple," Melody says.

"Yeah, we do, don't we?"

The elevator comes, shooting us up to the Penthouse floor, where we step off amid a crowd of costumed guests. The room is spacious, and from what Teresa told me earlier in the day, it is the reception area for the art galleries on the two levels below us.

Looking around, I can't help but laugh at some of the costumes. It seems as if all of the costumes I had suggested to Melody were in full effect. There are more than enough Draculas and Elviras. People are dressed as candy bars, clowns, monsters, mummies, and every movie character or celebrity you could think of from the past two years. There is even an Ike and Tina couple. We are clearly the most uniquely dressed individuals in the room as far as I can see. All of a sudden the two hundred I dropped on these costumes doesn't seem like a bad investment. We walk over to a small room marked as the coat-check room. There's no one to check the coats, so we walk in and place our coats on the hangers between other people's coats.

Smooth jazz plays throughout the large, dimly lit space, as people congregate at the bar or move to the dance floor to catch a slow two-step with their dates. There is a real mellow vibe throughout the place, and as we move through the crowd undetected, Melody's fingers interlock with mine.

"You want to get something to drink first?" she asks.

"Sure. What are you having, my queen?"

"A Cosmopolitan would be nice," she says.

"Really. I didn't know you drank Vodka."

"Well, Miles, there a lot of things you don't know about me," she says. "But if you stick around, you can get to know me a lot better."

Her smile causes me to smile. Then I remember the book on her nightstand about the two women meeting each week for Cosmos, and I ask, "Reading about it makes you want one?"

She smiles and responds, "You think you're smart, don't you?" She nudges me with her elbow.

I order Melody a Cosmo and myself a Singapore Sling, and we toast to getting to know each other better.

Just then I hear someone calling my name. I turn around to see Jean-Claude and Teresa Baptiste dressed as lions, Jean-Claude with a red-brownish mane hovering over his long, manicured dreadlocks, and Teresa with her face painted like that of a lioness and her little lion ears affixed to the top of her head. Jean-Claude has on the lion suit with a tail hanging down just above the backs of his knees; Teresa has on a beige cat body suit with a tail affixed to the back. Up until now, I had no idea that Teresa was so well built beneath the conservative clothing that she wears at work. She has the firm body of a dancer: strong legs, a flat stomach, and a sculpted upper body. I almost forget that my hand is interlocked with Melody's as the Baptistes approach us.

"Miles Thompson!" Jean-Claude says, gripping my hand and pulling me into an embrace as if we were the best of friends.

"Jean-Claude, it's good to see you again," I respond, attempting to match his enthusiasm.

As Jean-Claude greets Melody, Teresa reaches out to hug me and kiss me on my cheek. "Very original costume," she says. "I must say that you and Melody are probably going to win the prize this evening for best costumes."

"Thanks, but don't ever underestimate the power of lions."

"You can say that again, brother!" Jean-Claude says

in his rhythmic accent, pulling playfully at Teresa's lioness ears. "I told Teresa earlier that the lion is all about strength."

Observing the two of them together, they seem like complete opposites: Teresa, the reserved teacher, and Jean-Claude, the over-the-top charismatic playwright.

"You are truly beautiful in that costume," Teresa says complimenting Melody. "If I didn't know better, I would think you were actually Nefertiti."

"Thank you," Melody responds. "Not many women could pull off your costume either. You're in wonderful shape."

Jean-Claude looks at me and says, "See what happens when we leave the women alone to talk for a minute? They get to complimenting each other to death."

"Don't hate," Teresa says in a mocking voice, reminiscent of the students at our school.

We all laugh, as we walk on to the other side of the room to find a table to sit down and finish our drinks.

AFTER ANOTHER ROUND OF DRINKS, JEAN-CLAUDE has launched into telling us about a play that he's working on. The story centers around an incident where a well-to-do buppie on the rise commits suicide by leaping through the atrium of a downtown hotel just when it seems his life is perfect. All three acts trace the course of the man's life and the confusion resulting from his untimely death. It's definitely not good cocktail conversation, but Jean-Claude doesn't seem to be aware of Teresa shifting uncomfortably in her seat. Then, as if on cue, he looks over my shoulder and says, "Hey, that's Meredith Wilson with the Brooklyn Museum. They are putting together a Basquiat exhibit for next spring. I need to run over and talk to her for a minute. Excuse me."

Jean-Claude leaves the table, while the three of us continue nursing our cocktails. I feel Melody press her hand down on mine as she rises from her seat.

"I have to go powder my nose," she says.

I smile. I haven't heard a woman say that in a long time. "Sure," I say.

Before she slips away, I catch her lightly by the wrist and pull her closer to me. She leans down as I whisper in her ear, "Why don't we catch the next cab to Harlem and use these costumes for our own private party?"

She smiles at me and nods. "I'll be ready in a moment. You get the coats."

As Melody walks away, I lean across the table toward Teresa, who hasn't moved much since Jean-Claude walked away, and tell her that Melody and I are about to leave.

"So soon?" Teresa says.

"Yeah, it's getting a little late, and we've had a few drinks, so we're going to wind it down for the night."

"Well, I'm glad you guys came out."

I stand up, and Teresa offers to walk with me over to the coat-check room.

"You know, last year they didn't have as big a turnout as they did tonight. The Whitehall Foundation has been doing these for the last five years, and I think this has been the largest one yet."

"Really?"

We enter the room, now overflowing with coats. I reach through the stacks of leather jackets, pea coats, trench coats, furs, and shawls to get Melody's coat and my own.

"Miles, you look really handsome tonight," I hear Teresa say softly from behind me.

I turn to face her. "You were far from bad yourself."

"You like my costume?"

At this point I realize that we're alone in the room and the door is closed, me and this very beautiful woman clad only in a beige body suit.

"We really should get out of here," I say, moving toward the door, which is surprisingly farther away than I remember. "I wouldn't want Melody or Jean-Claude to get suspicious and start wondering where we are."

Teresa quickly steps into my path. "Miles, you're attracted to me, aren't you? I mean, I could be wrong but I feel like I'm getting a vibe from you."

"This isn't really the time or place to talk about this."

I listen to myself. I sound like some kind of choirboy, as if I had never had a risqué past. It's like the old men always say, "I might be old, but I'm not blind." And Teresa looks amazing. Her skin is so smooth and inviting that I have to pause and breathe. Any other place, any other time, maybe, but it's too much for my plate tonight.

Teresa steps forward, and something tells me to back away, but I surrender almost too easily with nothing but coats behind me. She presses her body against mine, and I just look at her. Slowly one of her hands eases up around my head, as she runs her other hand down my chest. My costume is doing very little to conceal my growing erection, and she quickly finds it, gripping it through the fabric. I close my eyes for a moment as I feel Teresa's mouth softly envelope my neck.

As I open my eyes to re-center myself, I see Melody

standing in the doorway with tears welling up in her eyes. I have no idea how long she's been standing there.

"Melody," I say, quickly moving away from Teresa. Then I say the most clichéd thing I could possibly say at a moment like this: "It's not what you think!"

Scarily composed, Melody turns around without saying a word and walks out, pushing the door closed behind her. My stomach is in my shoes by now, my erection a distant memory, and I am chasing after her with both coats dragging from my hands.

Trying to avoid a scene, I walk briskly through the room into the lobby area where I see Melody waiting impatiently by the elevator. Seeing her dressed like an Egyptian queen, in the costume that I picked out for her, hurts me to my heart. All she wanted to do was make me happy, and I realize at that exact moment if I can survive the damage of what has just happened, I will make a complete and total commitment to this woman.

"She came on to me," I say briskly. "I didn't do anything. I didn't touch her."

Melody ignores me, turning her back to me as the elevator arrives. I step on the elevator with her.

"Please say something," I say. "This is just a misunderstanding. We can work our way through this if we just talk about it."

Finally she looks at me. "I knew that she was interested in you. I could tell by the way she looked at you all night. I just thought that we had something special and that you wouldn't throw it up in my face like that. I haven't felt this disrespected since my husband cheated on me!" Tears begin to stream down her face. "You made a fool out of me up there! But I guess I made a fool out of myself thinking that I could have something real with you."

The elevator is letting us out on the lobby level before I have a chance to process the whole situation. Everything seems entirely surreal.

"I mean," she continues. "Why should you be any different from any of the other men that I've dated? You're just being a man. But ooh, it just hurts so damn bad!" she shouts, unable to control her emotions for a moment.

I reach out to hold her, to pull her closer so she can feel the depth of my feelings, but she pushes away from me and says in a voice as cold as ice, "Don't touch me."

She snatches her coat from my hand and storms out into the cool night.

"Melody, we just need to talk. I really care about you. You know I'd never do anything to mess up what we have."

She holds out her hand to hail a cab. Within seconds one pulls up to the curb in front of the building.

By this time I am pleading with Melody. "Baby, I need you to listen to me. I only want to be with you. I want us to be together. Just you and me."

She places one foot inside of the cab and looks at me, her eyes streaked in eyeliner. "You ain't said two words to me."

The cab pulls off with me standing paralyzed in the cool air. I want to hail a cab and follow Melody to her house, but I dismiss the thought. She probably needs some space right now, and it would be difficult to talk to her with her emotions so high.

I know I can't go back upstairs because that situation would be too awkward, so I reluctantly hail a cab to go back home.

Reflecting over what has just happened, I'm sobered even further by the fact that, even in an emotional crisis like this, Melody was classy enough to not make a scene upstairs.

I don't know how I'm going to face Teresa on Monday, but she's the least of my problems. I just want Melody back. As each minute passes, I realize that the feelings I have for Melody are much stronger than I previously allowed myself to believe.

19

OCTOBER 30, 2004

JA KENDRICK BROWN

I feel OK when I step out the restroom at Port Authority, but I woulda rather had the luxury of getting a shower at the crib. I'm a master of the "ho scrub" though (washing up under the arms and between the legs), and I always make sure I smell good and that I keep my hands clean. Back in the day, I learned that most females ain't with the dirty-ass fingernails shit. I had a girl tell me one time that it looked like I had been scratching dirt. And with me being a piano dude and all, I can't have people looking at my hands and thinking I'm some grimy-ass nigga. I don't mind being a little thugged out with the kicks and all, but my hands are the key to my survival. Gotta take care of the hands.

I'm rocking a hooded sweatshirt, a South Pole bubble down goose jacket, a pair of jeans and my Tims. My dreads are hanging, and I'm sporting a pair of shades, more to block out the wind and the Saturday sun blasting down on the sidewalks than for profiling.

It's been a while since I was ever this geeked about hollering at a girl. I've only really had one girlfriend before, and I dated her for two years. Since then, I've just been hollering at a honey here and there, but not really trying to catch feelings or get down with anybody on the relationship tip. But there's something about Lei Morgan that's just got me out there wide open. She seems like she's good people, and she's a definite dime piece. And maybe there's just a hint of what my man B.I.G. said about dating the quintessential R&B chick rolled up in there. Add it all up and you got why I'm trying to calm down as I head for the 2/3 train line.

I cop a seat in the middle of the car, next to the doors, and just focus on getting my breathing together. I find if I breathe slower, my heart rate slows and I shake off some of those nerves in the process. I do that most of the time before we perform on the trains, but I find myself needing to use the same thing now when I think about being one-on-one with Lei for the first time—outside of the studio and all the rah-rah that goes along with that whole industry scene. I just hope she's feeling me. Damn, I hope she's feeling me.

It's not long before the train stops at Houston, and I head over to our meeting spot. The DKNY/Statue of Liberty mural still looks fresh, like it was painted yesterday, but everything else has changed in the last few years. The gas station is gone. They built a building on what used to be a parking lot. I swear, if you stand still for too long, the City will change around you.

I take a look at my watch just to see how much time I have. It's almost ten in the morning. Trying to be *incognegro* in my shades, I glance to see if Lei is around. A couple of times I think I see her, but it's not her, just some girls who look like her from a distance.

For a while I just watch people coming and going, cabs flying through the streets, buses roaring down Broadway, people just wandering all over the place.

When I think about it, the scene looks like an anthill after someone stepped on it.

I scan the crowd again, and this time I see Lei in a pink bubble goose down with a matching beanie. I ease up next to her before I speak.

"Hey you," I say, surprising her.

"Ja! How are you doing?" She turns toward me and hugs me tightly. "Sorry I'm late."

"No biggie," I say. "How did your shoot go?"

"I wasn't really feeling it. I hope the label goes with some of the other pictures we did two weeks ago."

"What was wrong with the shoot?"

"The outfits were too over-the-top, and the photographer was such an asshole."

I nod. "So when is the album dropping?"

"We're supposed to have a March release. Tangie, our manager, says that's good because the label will be just coming off the Christmas season and ready to crack some of the new acts." She looks around for a second. "You wanna get something to eat?"

"Sure."

The guys and I haven't hustled the trains in a minute, so I'm hoping that whatever we're gonna be eating fits in my limited budget. We wind up at a small café on a side street. Glancing at the menu, I think that this is something that I could safely swing for the day. Plus I don't want Lei to think I'm some broke-ass busta.

When we sit down, she says, "Just curious, but how old are you?"

"Huh?" I ask, wondering if my answer will shorten the date.

"How old are you, Ja?"

"How old do I look?"

"About sixteen or seventeen."

"Really," I say, trying not to sound impressed that I look older than my age.

"So how old are you?" she asks for the third time.

I start to lie to her, but I figure what the hell. "I'm fifteen, but I'll be sixteen in a few months."

"You're a baby!" she says.

Suddenly I feel the butterflies flapping wild as a motherfucker in my stomach. This date is about to be over before it even gets started.

"Well, how old are you?" I ask to shift the attention from myself.

"A real lady never reveals her age."

"Oh, I'm sorry," I offer.

After a moment, she smiles and says, "I'm sixteen."

Oh, shit. Here I am thinking that she must be a lot older than me to be calling me out like that. I chuckle 'cause now I get her joke.

Talking to her is a lot easier than I expected. She has a great sense of humor, and she's naturally fly—the kind of fly that don't really need no make-up. Her hair seems longer than it was the last time I saw her, but then again the last two times I saw her she was rocking the ponytail. Her caramel complexion is smooth and her lips are glossed in a natural-looking lipstick. I get nervous thinking about what it would be like to kiss them. Her eyes dance when she talks, and her smile is fly as hell. A few times I zone out on the conversation and lose myself in just looking at her.

For a moment my stomach cramps up when I realize millions of guys'll be out there trying to get at her after the album drops. All kinds of flashy niggas with ends. I realize that I don't even know what made her want to go out with me in the first place. I want to ask her, but I don't want to run the risk of sounding like I don't deserve to be here with her (although I kinda feel that way).

"Are you originally from New York?" she asks.

"Yeah. I been here my whole life. What about you?"

Nibbling on her sandwich, she says, "I grew up in Fairfax, Virginia, right outside of D.C. I moved here about three years ago because I wanted to go to LaGuardia for high school and wanted to already be here when I auditioned."

"So you're a student at LaGuardia?" I ask.

"Yes. I'll finish next year, so I'm hoping that this album really takes off."

"Man, that's nice," I say. Now I'm wishing I had actually followed through with the application and audition. I could've already known her by now, but hey, hindsight's a motherfucker. "You should do just fine. I heard some of your tracks while I was at the studio, and they're all blazing."

"Thanks."

Lei reaches across the table and takes my hands. I feel those butterflies again. She squeezes my hands slightly, and I realize that my hands are probably damp from being nervous as a hooker in church, but she don't let on.

"You have nice hands," she says. I wait for her to comment on the sweat, but she never does. "They're soft but strong. No rough spots. You don't do a lot of hard labor do you?"

I'm not sure of what she's getting at. "I'm a musician. My hands are made for playing the piano."

She laughs and puts my hands back on the table. "You're so cute."

Now I'm feeling like a little kid who doesn't do any hard work, but when I see the look in her eyes, I know that she's not trying to diss me at all; she's just flirting. I smile back.

We leave the restaurant, and Lei tells me that she's gotta get back to the Upper West Side and meet up with her group. I walk her to the corner where she starts trying to hail a cab. Immediately I start trying to think of how I can get a kiss from her before she breaks out. I have no idea of when I'll see her again, but she tells me to just call her sometime. A cab approaches and begins to slow down, and I'm starting to feel like my window of opportunity is closing up.

She steps up to the cab, and I open the door. As she stands in the doorway, she turns back to face me, and I walk toward her. My Tims feel like big ass cement blocks.

"Thanks for lunch, Ja."

"Well, hopefully we can do it again—soon."

I step closer to her, and she reaches out to hug me. As she pulls me closer, I feel her kiss my cheek, and a glow comes over me. I watch as she sits down, and I close the door, waiving to her as the cab pulls off.

Watching the cab turn the corner, I realize the rest of my day is wide open. I walk to a payphone and call Yusef's house. He's not home, so I call Quent's house. He's not home either. Then I call my sister who doesn't even try to answer the phone, which probably means Daryl is over there. With so much time left in the day, I head to Sam Ash's. At least I can be practicing on a piano, maybe even write a song for our future album.

20

OCTOBER 30, 2004

LEI MORGAN

As my cab zooms past building after building, headed back toward Midtown, I think of Ja, and how fine he is. He's got that kind of hard, bad boy look, but I can see in his eyes that he's got a softer side to him. He seems like a genuine guy who's really trying to do something with his life. His height also doesn't hurt anything because I have a thing for the tall, slim type.

When I met him at the studio, I could tell that he was feeling me. It seemed like he was scoping me the entire time I was there. Tasha Jenkins, one of the members of Deja Ice, joned me the rest of the afternoon after the guys had already left.

"Mr. Dreadlocks was all up in your grill, girl!"

I played it off. "Well, don't blame him for having good taste."

"Well, go ahead with your little fast ass. Get you some of that tall Rasta man!" Tasha joked.

"Don't front, girl," I said. "You know he got some flava."

Tasha nodded while still laughing. "He a'ight, I guess."

I was glad that Ja finally got up with me because I was starting to think I would have to count him out. Niggas try to get at me everyday, and in the industry there's always someone trying to sweeten the deal with this or that. I'm not that kind of chick, but all the same, time stops for no man (or woman), so if you wanna holler, you have to step up.

He seemed nervous when we first hooked up, but by the time we finished eating, he was pretty relaxed. At one point, I reached over and grabbed his hands. They just looked so nice. You just don't catch guys who have nice hands like that. I wanted to touch them. I imagined what it would feel like to have his hands touching me, so I made the first move. I think he liked that.

He was also a gentleman, picking up the ticket on lunch. I know a lot of niggas who would've kicked the bill over to me just because I have a record deal. It's nice to know that chivalry is not entirely dead.

As I stepped in the cab, I started to kiss Ja on the lips, but I wanted to leave a little mystery, something to be desired, so I kissed him on his cheek. He's a nice guy, and I would like to go out with him again, so I want to make sure we do all of this the right way and take it slow.

Now as the cab pushes through the City, my cell phone starts ringing.

"Hello," I say, fumbling with the earpiece.

"Lei, where you at? We're gonna be late for the party!" Tangie yells into the phone.

The party doesn't start until seven, but to Tangie everything is urgent.

"I'm on my way right now. Don't blow a gasket."

"I swear, you girls run me crazy!"

"You run yourself crazy, Tangie," I say, stifling my laughter.

Hanging up the phone, I have to smile. Three years ago, I would have never imagined that I'd have a record deal. Moving to New York and staying with my cousin was one of the smartest moves I ever made. My parents were afraid to let me leave Fairfax, Virginia, to go to school up here. Because my father worked in marketing over at AOL in Dulles and my mother taught eighth grade science over at a middle school in Oakton, they felt that I should have looked to DC if I were trying to do something that Fairfax County didn't offer. After going back and forth on the subject for three months, my older cousin, Liz DeBerry, came to my rescue by offering me a place to stay and assuring my parents that it was all cool for me to apply to LaGuardia since it had a strong reputation.

I met Tasha Jones and Charlotte Watkins at LaGuardia, and since all of us were specializing in voice, we quickly found a common ground and decided to form a group. We got our big break when we performed at an open mike down in Alphabet City one night. That's when we met Tangie, a "large and in charge" brown skinned sister with a low haircut and the energy of five men. She sweet-talked us into letting her be our manager by saying that she could get us a deal within a year. She didn't lie either. She turned around and got us a demo done and passed it on to her off-and-on again boyfriend, Smoke-T. Smoke-T passed it along to Terrell Bonds, and we got signed two months later to Big Business Records.

Honestly, everything has happened so quickly that at times I feel like I have gotten lost in the hustle and bustle of things. Because of how hectic things have been, I've been avoiding the dating scene for a minute. I don't know what made me change my mind for Ja. Maybe I was overdue for a little male companionship.

I have absolutely no idea of what I want to see

happen with this situation, but if he can deal with all this craziness around me and Deja Ice and keep a level head about his own success, we could definitely chill. And that would be nice.

21

OCTOBER 30, 2004

MILES THOMPSON

I couldn't even get out of bed this morning. I woke up around 8:30 and stared at the clock for a few minutes before I remembered what happened last night. After leaving three messages, I gave up on calling Melody and went back to sleep. Now I'm lying on the top of my comforter in a t-shirt and a pair of boxers, too frustrated and tired to move. Thank God it's a Saturday.

The curtains in my room are drawn tightly, so it's completely dark. The light flashing from my phone as it rings on the nightstand next to my bed is the only sign of any activity. I reach over and sluggishly pick it up after the third ring.

"Hello," I say, praying that Melody's voice will respond on the other end. If I had the inclination, I probably could have just checked the caller ID before answering the phone, but that would have been too much like right.

"Miles, wake your sleepy ass up!" Richard Hardiman says playfully.

I sit up lazily in my bed, adjusting the phone. "Richard, what's going on?"

"Damn, man. You sound like someone just ran over your dog or something. You all right?"

"Man, if you only knew the half."

"Hold on. Let me get situated and put on my 'Miles Drama' hat. OK. Talk to your boy. What's going on up there? Do I need to go up there and kick somebody's ass?"

I sit up on the edge of my bed, placing my head against my left hand, while my right hand cradles the phone against my face. I can't remember how long I've been lying in bed, and because the room is so dark, I'm clueless as to what it looks like outside.

"My new lady friend cut me loose last night."

"New friend? Hell, Miles, I was just there a few weeks ago. How did you meet someone that fast?"

"This is New York, man. Your life can change in a day here."

"I got you. Keep going."

"We've been dating for a few weeks, and to be completely honest with you, I really care about this woman. She's so unique and beautiful and smart and sexy, and best of all, I think that she was really into who I am as a person."

"I feel you," Richard says. "So what happened to shut all of that down?"

"One of my female co-workers made a move on me in the coat-check room at a party last night, and she walked in on it."

"Damn. She caught another woman pushing up on you?"

"Yep."

"What did you do?"

"I told her that it wasn't what it looked like." I grimace admitting this part.

"Oh, hell, no. I've been off the market for about

fifteen years, but I can tell you that was a bad move." He chuckles. "And this co-worker of yours, is she fine?"

"Is she?" I say matter-of-factly. "She is definitely a brick house, but she's married."

"Hold up. Are you saying that your woman walked in on you getting down with a married woman?"

I shake my head. It sounds even worse hearing it come from Richard.

"Well, I didn't do anything. She came on to me, touching and kissing."

"Damn," Richard says. "You kissed her?"

"Technically speaking."

"Either you did or you didn't. Well, let me ask you this: Did your dick get hard?"

"Richard, come on, man!"

"OK. Well, you're definitely in the doghouse. If she was ugly you might have been able to talk your way out of it, but this co-worker of yours was sexy so I know you were standing at attention like Colin Powell —and so does your lady friend. See, what she's thinking is that if she had shown up a few minutes later, you might have had your co-worker spread out over some coats."

I exhale into the phone. I hate to admit it, but Richard has a point. I don't think I would have necessarily gone that far with Teresa, but is that something that I would expect Melody to know?

"Plus," Richard continues, "I knew you from the time you were a skinny-ass freshman with a big ass head. Back in the day, before Bettina, you had chicks spreading like peanut butter. The life of an R&B singer, I guess." He laughs.

"So any ideas for what a brother could do to get everything back on track?"

Richard has been my sounding board for so long

that it seems instinctual to ask him his thoughts when my own mind is too broken down to think.

"That's going to take some time and a lot of persistence on your part. How close were the two of you?"

"Pretty close, man. I actually want something exclusive with her," I say. I feel emotionally weakened by this admission, but I don't know why.

"Well, all I can say is you have to continue to let that show in how you deal with her."

"I've called three times this morning already."

"Yeah. You got it pretty bad."

I stand up and stretch with the phone nestled between my ear and shoulder.

"You love her?" he asks, and for the first time in a while I'm speechless, but not because I'm offended by the question.

"So what's up on your end?" I ask, attempting to shift gears in the conversation.

Sensing my change, he says, "Oh, yeah. I was just calling to see if you were going to make it to the house warming in a few weeks."

"What house warming?"

"Didn't you get the invitation I sent out at the beginning of October?" he asks.

"No."

"Dammit, I knew I should have just mentioned it to you when I saw you the last time. Must have sent it to the wrong address or something. Anyway, Erica and I are hosting a house warming party for the new house we bought in Marietta back in July. We're having over a few of our close friends and family since everyone seems to be going in different directions for Thanksgiving. It should be nice, so make sure you mark your calendar for November 13th."

I can't even remember what I have to do tomorrow, let alone a few weeks from now. Nothing comes to mind in terms of my schedule, so I agree to make the trip. Honestly, I haven't been back to Atlanta since I left, and if it weren't for Richard's invitation, I would probably hold off on going back for a while longer.

"How is everything else going with you, Miles?" Richard asks.

"Work is going all right," I respond. Then I remember Ja Kendrick. "Richard, I met this kid. I think he's a piano prodigy or something. And he's from Harlem."

"Really? How old is he?"

"About fifteen. He reads music at a professional level, and I think, seriously, he's better than me. Both of his parents are deceased, and he lives with a sister who I don't believe is doing much in the way of caring for him. He's a great kid though. Great future ahead of him."

"Man, that's really something. How did you meet him?"

"He was panhandling on the train with his friends and they performed one of my songs. And they did an amazing job! Anyway, I ran into him again a few days later at a music shop and invited him to come by and visit with me over at TMA. He came through, and we had a pretty good time. I expect he'll probably come through more often so he can play around on the piano in my classroom."

I start to tell Richard about how I had started back having the nightmares and how after I actually connected with Ja Kendrick the nightmares stopped. I know he would just suggest I go back to see another therapist. It's not that I have anything against therapy, but I just feel that the last time I committed to a series of sessions, I didn't really accomplish a lot. I spent more time answering questions I could have asked myself than I did getting anything more substantial.

Maybe it was the therapist; maybe it was me. At the end of the day, I'm primarily concerned about making sure I can look myself in the mirror, get a good night's sleep, and be able to move forward with my life.

Richard shakes me from my thoughts. "Well, it sounds like you have a lot of stuff going on in your life right now. If you need me for anything, don't hesitate to holler."

"Thanks," I say.

"You know I love you like a red-headed stepbrother."

We laugh as we get off the phone. Placing the phone back on the base, I rest my head in my hands and massage my temples. Why am I being so emotional about all of this? Easy come, easy go, right? That's probably the reason I didn't go into law, business, or some other field where you use logic, as opposed to emotion. I know, as an artist, that I tend to be an emotionally driven man. I can't just look at things totally through the lenses of logic. When I fall for a woman, I fall hard. The thing is that I usually don't let my guard down enough to let anyone into my life who could put me in this type of situation. Melody must have just slipped in under the radar.

WHEN I WAS JUST A SOPHOMORE IN COLLEGE, MY life was changed forever. I had hopped in the little Volkswagon Beetle I had just bought from some white boy out in Lithia Springs, Georgia, and had decided to drive home to Tupelo, Mississippi, to say hello to my parents for the weekend. When I pulled up at my house, a small yellow three-bedroom structure tucked away off of Main Street, I jumped out and ran to the door.

My mother emerged from the sitting room with a giant smile on her face. She was beautiful, her hair neatly pressed down to her shoulders and her reading glasses still perched on the bridge of her nose. She was pushing fifty but didn't look it at all. She embraced me heartily as I came through the door.

"Miles, I'm surprised to see you!" She squeezed me again and then looked around behind me. "How did you get here?"

"I drove!" I said excitedly. "Look over there. I just bought a car!"

She stepped out onto the porch and looked over at my used Beetle. "You bought your first car," she said, with a sense of pride in her voice. "You must have played a lot of gigs to get that much money."

"Well, maybe a few. I got a good deal on it, though."

Mom had always wanted Pops and her to buy me a car, but money was never right around the house. With Pops working long hours at the factory and Mom teaching social studies out at a small county school, there just never seemed to be enough money floating around for them to buy it.

"You hungry?" she asked, as I stepped through the front door.

"Oh, yes, ma'am."

"Well, we have some left over fried chicken, cabbage, cornbread, green beans, and sweet potato casserole in the fridge."

I went in, heated everything, and fixed myself a big plate before sitting down at the dining room table. Mom came over and sat down beside me. "You're looking good," she told me. "Looks like you've been doing a lot of exercising."

I blushed. "Well, you know. I'm trying to look the part up there."

As I ate about a third of the food on my plate, I asked Mom, "Where's Pops? He still at work?"

"You know your father. They switched his schedule around at the plant so many times that most of the day he's always at work. He'll be happy to see you, though. Just this morning, before he left for work, he was telling me how proud he was of you holding on to the music scholarship."

"Really?" I say. "That's cool."

I ate the rest of the food on my plate and decided to take my Beetle for a little cruise around the town. Now that I had wheels, I could let the fine young women in town see that I was coming up since I had started college.

If I'd stayed at home and chatted longer with Mom, my life probably would have never changed much from what it was already becoming, but some- times things happen so coincidentally that it must not have even been a coincidence at all. And if that's the case, then I was destined to come apart at the seams early in the evening of that Friday as I rolled through the streets of Tupelo.

At first I couldn't tell it was him because he wasn't in his work uniform. But he was the right height and build. He had a beard sprinkled with the salt and pepper look that came with age, but I wasn't totally sure if it was really him. Walking just ahead of him into the bar was a very tall and attractive younger woman dressed in a tight black dress. He ushered her through the door on the side street rather quickly—quickly enough for me to double back and park my car out in front of the bar.

The sign on the bar read "Cecil's Lounge." Growing up, that bar was where all of the drunks, loose women, and guys with a little extra overtime money in their pockets went to get laid or liquored. I had never been in Cecil's before because I never had a reason to go—until now.

I walked through the door and looked around in the dark, damp room filled with cigarette smoke and grungy Negroes looking to escape their own lives for a few hours. There was nothing classy about the spot. This was the kind of place you told your kids to steer clear of. This was the kind of place that could drag the property value of the entire block down. This was the kind of place that in the mid-80s would turn into a drug haven and come to epitomize the area known as "the bad side of town." But back then in the mid-seventies, it was still several years from realizing its awful fate.

I looked around in the dark room, adjusting my eyes to the minimal glow of the red and black lights that lined the walls. For a minute I couldn't see where he had gone, but then I made out his shape at a table tucked away in the back. I stared at him for a minute, my legs weak, my hands sweaty. My face flushed hot, but I knew I was walking over there.

When I arrived at the table, his back was turned to me as he necked with the woman I had seen come in directly in front of him.

"Excuse me," I said, as calmly as I could muster. "Let me holler at you for a second." I tapped him on his shoulder.

My father turned to face me. His face filled with horror as he stood up and followed me over to a table across the room.

Seeing that man cheating on my mother out in public sickened me to my stomach. I was angry and sad at the same time. It was as if someone had died. My parents were always the perfect couple, always in church, doing things in the community. But here my father was looking pathetic and busted in a cheap ass bar.

"Pops, what are you doing?" I whispered to him, trying to contain my anger.

He just looked at me. He probably wanted to know how I found him there, how I had gotten back from Georgia and caught him with his hand deep inside the cookie jar.

"Mom is at home right now thinking about you, and you're all up in this place with that tramp over there. What the fuck is your problem?" It was the first and last time I had ever cursed at my father.

He didn't respond. If the circumstances had been different, he would have whipped me with his belt—even at my age. But that day, he was emasculated. He was just some punk nigger who was jiving on my mother. He was just a funky zero who couldn't even say anything. My father wasn't shit.

I asked him one more question. "What do you want me to do, Pops? Huh?"

With eyes that reflected a weakness I had never seen in any man, he looked at me and said, "Just leave!"

I stared back at him, and I couldn't believe that my father was going to return back to the table with that heifer and pretend that I had never busted him. And like that, my father ambled back across the room to the booth where I had discovered him. I stood up for a moment, and I felt like screaming something across the room at him, anything. I stood there by that table for what seemed like hours until finally I could feel tears easing down my cheeks.

I walked back to my car and sat down for a moment. I couldn't go back home to Mom like this. I knew how much she loved Pops. I didn't want to destroy her world with what I had just discovered, although I seriously thought against it as the tears washed down my face. I felt as if I was betraying her by not telling her what I had found out, but I rationalized that it wasn't my place to tell her. Pops had to own up to that on his own.

I had nothing left to say to him after that. I wasn't going back into the bar, and I couldn't bring myself to go home, so I got onto US-78, headed toward Birmingham, with the intention of never speaking to my father again. To this day, I still have had very little to say to him.

I BELIEVE THAT'S THE REASON I NEVER STEPPED out on Bettina and Travis. I would never have wanted my son to be able to think the same thing of me as I think of my old man. It was hard, though, because I had gotten married at the height of The Triumph's fame. I was being bombarded with women from every angle while I was on tour, but the thought of my sorry-ass father sitting in that bar always sickened me to the thought of being with anyone other than my wife. What's even funnier is that I did love Bettina; I was just never *in love* with her. There were never any butterflies. There was never the desire to lock myself in the bedroom with her on a Saturday and make love to her until we were both unconscious from exhaustion. She was like a friend who was cool, but not the best friend that I had always imagined that I would have when I got married.

After the divorce, I lay low for a while and got myself together. In fact, Melody is the first person I had actually felt strongly enough about to want to commit to. She has all of the qualities that I've ever wanted in a woman, including a number of qualities I never knew to put on the list. That's why the whole situation is really bothering me. I could see if I had really done something to her, but I feel like I'm just being punished for a crime I didn't commit, and I'm not being allowed to plead my case before being sentenced.

My mind continues to race with these thoughts as I step out of my apartment to get a bite to eat from JuJu's Coco Bread spot down in Brooklyn. I haven't been out of the apartment all day, so the idea of taking the express train down through Manhattan doesn't really bother me. The sun set several hours ago, and the sky is approaching the depths of darkness. I'm just glad that JuJu's closes at midnight on Saturdays. I glance down at my watch, and I see that it's nearly ten o'clock, which gives me enough time to get down there and get my order in before they close.

As I walk into the Metro Station I think about what I'm going to order. Curry chicken? Goat? Ox tails? Patties? My mouth is watering from the possibilities. I haven't been there in a while, and with the way that I've been feeling today, I feel that treating myself to a nice Caribbean meal is not too much to ask, even if it is going to be take-out tonight.

I'm not waiting very long before the A train pulls up. I grab a seat on the last car and reach in my trench coat pocket for my iPod earphones. I flip randomly through my playlists until I find something mellow to listen to. My earphones fill with the sounds of Ramsey Lewis and Earth, Wind & Fire performing their song "Sun Goddess." My mood softens some, as I find my head nodding rhythmically to the beat.

The train car is nearly empty, except for a Dominican couple sitting down from me and a guy lying down on the last seat asleep. As I notice the guy's Timberland hiking boots stretched out over the edge of the seat and his dreadlocks stretched across his brown face, I rise to my feet and walk cautiously toward him.

"Ja," I say softly, tapping him on his shoulder. "Ja."

His eyes open slowly as he registers who I am.

"You all right?" I ask.

He looks at me, his eyes still dazed from sleep, and slowly sits up in his seat. "Miles," he says, his voice ringing with exhaustion. "What's up?"

"It's not safe sleeping on the trains like this. Are you heading home right now?" I ask.

He looks at me confused. "Huh?"

"Are you on your way home?" I ask again.

"Oh," he says. "No. I can't go home tonight." And then he whispers, "I'm just going to catch a little nap on the train and get back out there in the morning."

"Get back out where?" I ask.

"You know. The City."

I swallow hard when the thought hits me that Ja Kendrick's probably been riding the trains for a while now, catching sleep whenever he could get it. I suspected things weren't all that great at home for him, but I never suspected that the kid was virtually homeless.

"Are you hungry?" I ask. "I'm on my way to pick up some curry and cocoa bread from JuJu's in Brooklyn. I could appreciate the company."

Wiping his eyes, a smile spreads across his face. "Sure. I could eat."

22

OCTOBER 30-31, 2004

JA KENDRICK BROWN

I'm standing at the counter of JuJu's checking out the panel of chalkboards above my head. They have all kinds of combos written on them. My mouth is watering like a motherfucker, and it hits me just how hungry I am. I don't remember eating after I bought lunch for Lei, so when I get to the window, I order a veggie patty, curry goat stew with rice, a side of plantains, a huge slab of coco bread, and a large soda.

I reach into my pocket to pull out some cash from my steadily shrinking wad, and Miles stops me and pulls out his own wallet. I thank him, and move down the counter to wait on the food.

Monday I've got to get back to hustling the trains. We been slacking off, waiting for all this music stuff to come through with Big Business Records, but, truth be told, I need some ends now. Working the trains is the only income I got coming in, and I don't wanna go back to being broke and out on my ass. I ain't got anyone to take care of me, so I have to take care of my-self. The only gig I have is these trains, so I need to make sure to call Yusef tomorrow to make sure we're gonna be getting up Monday after school.

"Order 103," a big, light-skinned woman calls out,

while ringing a bell on the ledge of the kitchen window.

Miles steps up and grabs the big bag of food. I can smell all of the spices through the wrappers. I'm so hungry I could suck the flavor out the damn bag.

He glances at his watch and looks at me. "I was originally going to take the food home and eat, but we have about half an hour before they close if you want to eat here."

Part of me wants to kill all of that food right now, but the survivor-side of me wants to go back to Miles's crib, because I think it'd be easier for me to convince him to let me crash there tonight. A couch is a hell of a long way from the hard plastic seats of the A train. Plus, you ain't gotta worry about waking up every five minutes to keep an eye out for people trying to rob you.

"Let me just grab a little bit of that coco bread, and we can take it back to your crib."

He nods and sifts through the bag. He hands me a big ass slab of coco bread wrapped in wax paper. It's warm and soft, like a towel fresh out the dryer, and when I bite into it, my head starts swimming.

We catch a gypsy cab back to Harlem, while munching on whatever we can manage to keep from spilling in the backseat.

"So, Ja," Miles says. "You must have had a busy day."

"Yeah. I been at it for a while."

"What'd you do?"

The food slowly starts to fill my belly, and I feel more relaxed. Miles is real cool for hooking me up with this meal. I know within the hour I'll probably be laid out from what Mama used to call "the itis", sleeping on a full stomach. I think back to what I was doing earlier. "I had a date this morning. Her name is Lei Morgan."

"Lei? That's a nice name."

"Yeah," I say. "She's a singer. She's with this group called Deja Ice, and they have an album dropping next spring. Oh man, she's so fine!"

I get excited just thinking about her.

"I'll bet she is," Miles says. "I can't see you smiling like that over a girl who was less than that. How did you meet her?"

"We were over at the Big Business studio by Port Authority, and she was there with her group."

"I see the music business is paying off for you already," he says, laughing. "So how did your date go?"

I can't help but smile 'til I feel my cheeks starting to hurt. "Awesome."

I think about her holding my hands, and I remember the feel of her kiss when she said goodbye. "She's perfect."

"That's a great feeling," Miles says, looking away through the car window, almost like something depressed him just now. I wanna ask him what's wrong, but just then he starts back talking. "I know it's kind of late, so if you want to sleep at my apartment, you're welcome to. The couch in the den lets out into a bed."

I do everything in my power to play it cool. I am so fucking relieved I don't have to go back to the trains tonight. I wanna shake his hand, but instead I just nod and say, "Thanks."

I WAKE UP THE NEXT MORNING TO THE SMELL OF scrambled eggs, sausage, grits, and biscuits. Definitely not a New York breakfast. I don't think I've had a breakfast like this is in a minute, since some time before Auntie Sarah got sick. After Mama passed, different people in the family would cook for us. Auntie

Sarah did most of the cooking, and that wasn't all that often. Before Sherita got strung out, she would chip in and do some work, too.

"Good morning," Miles says when I walk into the kitchen.

I wipe some of the sleep out my eyes. "Good morning."

This man has stuff laid out everywhere, but I can't complain 'cause it looks like I'll be two for two on getting fed.

"I want to talk to you for a minute. Have a seat at the table," he says, pointing to a chair at the table.

I walk over and sit down. I don't know what the hell to expect. I wait for him to unload.

"I want you to be straight up with me. What is your situation at home?"

I look down for a moment 'cause I ain't ready to look him in the eyes yet. I ain't sure how much I want to tell him. I wanna just eat, but I know Miles is probably waiting for me to start talking before he turns me loose on the food.

The longer I sit at the table, the scent of the food whipping at my nose, the more I wonder why I don't just open up to this man who seems for real about helping me.

I give in.

"I stay in the apartment I grew up in with my sister, Sherita," I say.

He nods, waiting for me to go on.

"My mother died back when I was little, and I ain't never know my father. My sister and me just been making ends meet for the last few years."

Miles starts fixing two plates of food. "Tell me more about your sister," he says, as he piles up food on one of the plates and sits it down in front of me.

"Well, she's twenty-three." I feel funny talking

about my sister 'cause the whole situation with her is just so fucked up.

"Does she work?"

"No, sir. She don't think she need a job. She got a boyfriend."

"And what does he do?"

"He's a dough boy."

"A what?"

"He sells drugs, sir."

My sister is a drug addict, I tell myself. Why is that so hard to admit to someone else?

"So your sister is involved with a drug dealer, and he takes care of her," Miles repeats.

"My sister's on drugs," I blurt out. Now it's all out there. I don't know exactly how Miles is gonna act, but he don't look too shook.

"So you've been trying to hold everything together, but I take it your sister's boyfriend is probably taking over your apartment and that's causing you some problems of your own." Miles places his plate down on the table and he pauses to bless the food. "So you sleep on the train to get away from your sister's boyfriend?"

"Yeah. I guess you could say that," I say.

I stick a forkful of eggs into my mouth and bite into a strip of crispy bacon. My eyes start watering as I look at my food.

"Are you all right?" Miles asks.

He reaches over and slides a box of Kleenex in front of me.

When he says that, something in me just busts wide open, and I start crying like a baby. I cry like I ain't cried in the last five years and I'm making up for lost time. I'm scared by how heavy my voice is and how all of these tears are choking my ability to breathe.

Miles steps around the table and kneels down in front of me. I can't bring myself to look at him through my blurred eyes. Suddenly, he reaches out and hugs me. I collapse on his shoulder and cry harder than I've ever cried in my life. I cry for Mama who left me and Sherita alone to fend for ourselves in this fucked up world; I cry for Sherita, who couldn't deal with the pressure of being a parent to me and had to turn to drugs; I cry because I miss my Auntie Sarah; I cry because sometimes the struggle to get by is just so damn hard, but I have to press forward anyway; and I cry because Melvin cared enough to try to help me out, in spite of all this bullshit in my life.

As I lift my head from his soaked shoulder, I feel like a kid looking into the eyes of his pops. "Miles, tell me what to do."

He pulls his chair around the table and sits down to face me. "Ja, for now, I want you to call your sister and let her know where you are. Then I'm going to take you by your apartment, and I want you to pick up whatever ever you need to pick up. You're going to stay here with me until we can get all of this other stuff on track. I'm not going to have you riding the trains every night. I can't sleep at night knowing that you're out there putting yourself in danger. I would have never let my son choose homelessness over a loving, caring environment." Miles pauses for a minute, and I wanna ask him about his own son. He continues matter-of-factly, "You don't have a problem staying here, do you?"

"No," I say.

"You're welcome to use anything in the apartment," he says. "I'll get you a key today."

I nod. My face is streaked with dried tears, but I still finish my plate.

We don't speak for the rest of breakfast.

AFTER BREAKFAST, I CALL SHERITA. THIS TIME SHE answers.

"Hey, sis.... Yeah.... I was calling to let you know that I'm gonna be staying with one of my friends for a few days, and I was about to come by and pick up some of my stuff."

I don't know why I'm even calling her to ask to do something that she's in no position to stop me from doing. Part of me wants to do this the right way; the other part wants to be sure that I'm not gonna run into Daryl while I'm over there. I just don't want Miles up in the mix on some bullshit like that.

I get off the phone with her, and Miles and I catch a cab over to my apartment, which is really not more than fifteen blocks away, going down a few streets and across a few avenues. When we get there Miles walks with me up the three flights to the apartment at the end of the hall. I open the door and call out, "Sherita, it's just me and my friend Miles."

I reach for a bag out the closet in the main room and start packing. I put Angela up against the couch so I don't forget her. My sister, who still hasn't moved from the bedroom, calls out for Miles's sake. "Excuse the apartment! It's been a rough week!"

"It's not a problem at all," Miles says.

While I grab a few things from the bathroom, my sister comes out of her bedroom wrapped in a silk robe, her hair wrapped in a dingy pink bandana. If she didn't look so much like a drug fiend, she might've been cute.

"Sherita Brown," she says to him, offering her hand.

Miles rises from his seat. "Miles Thompson. Nice to meet you."

"You look really familiar," she says. "Are you some-body famous or something?"

"I used to be a in a band called The Triumphs a while back."

Sherita smiles. "Yeah, now I remember you." She makes a flirtatious gesture with her hand, and it looks gross. "So what do you want with my little brother?"

"Well, your brother has asked me to work with him on his music, and I told him we could accomplish more if he stayed with me for a while."

"That sounds like some bullshit," she says.

It sounds like bullshit to me, too, but I can understand where Miles is coming from.

"Well, it might sound like bullshit, but it's the truth."

Sherita nods, seemingly impressed with Miles's ability to cuss back. "Well," she says. "You're welcome to visit for while."

"Thank you," he responds. "But we have to run a few errands this afternoon." For good measure, he adds, "You have a nice place, though. It's pretty spacious in here."

"Yeah, it's a'ight," she says, quickly losing interest in the conversation.

She starts scratching at her arms and twitching a little, and I can tell she's gonna be going back in her room to get a hit soon.

"Well, it was nice meeting you," Sherita says, as she walks away.

"Nice to meet you too," Miles offers.

He turns to me. "Are we ready?" he asks.

"Yep," I say, grabbing my duffle bag. He picks up Angela and we leave the apartment.

AFTER WE GET BACK TO MILES'S, I ASK TO USE THE

phone. I just wanna call Yusef and let him know how he can get at me for the next few days.

"Yo," he says, picking up after the second ring.

"Yo, this is Ja. Yusef?"

"Yeah, guy."

"What's up witcha?"

"You ain't heard?" he says. "I been trying to call you all day at your crib, but I couldn't get an answer."

"What? What happened?"

"Quent fucked us."

"What?" My heart starts to race like a motherfucker.

"Quent straight fucked us out the deal with Big Business."

I plop down on the couch. "Talk to me. Tell me exactly what's going on."

"I found this out yesterday. Apparently that nigga Quent went behind our backs and signed a production deal or something with Terrell, and then Terrell turned around and did the deal with Big Business. It all went down yesterday."

"What does that mean for us?" I ask.

"It means that Big Business decided not to go with a singing group and just put Quent with a producer to do a solo joint."

I'm already sitting on the couch, so I can't fall any lower. "What do we do now?"

"We call it a day. We're done."

"Shit." There's not much else I can think to say.

"But if I ever see that nigga on the streets, I'm gonna fuck him up on sight," Yusef says.

"Let me know if you find him, 'cause I want to put my foot in his little fat ass, too."

"Well, guy, I gotta roll out and go check on my grandmoms."

"One," I say, hanging up the phone.

Damn, Quent. Why did you have to go and fuck us? Now I feel stuck, like someone took a monster shit on my only dream and there ain't a damn thing I can do about it. I wanna cry for a moment, but it passes. I guess there's just too much in my life that's fucked up that if I started crying again, I'd probably never stop.

As I sit on the couch, Miles walks over and places a key on the coffee table in front of me.

"My home is now your home," he says.

I lift the key from the table and look at it, turning it around in my hand, and wonder what could possibly happen next.

THE THIRD MOVEMENT

23

OCTOBER 31, 2004

TERESA BAPTISTE

"Sweetie," I say, leaning over and rubbing Jean-Claude's back. "I'm going for a walk."

He barely acknowledges me as he stirs, half-asleep, beneath the thin rumpled sheet on the bed. I run my hand across his sculpted back, leaning over to kiss the side of his face that is exposed.

"OK," he mumbles, not bothering to open his eyes.

I grab my phone so that he can call me when he wakes up and forgets that I told him I was going for a walk.

As I step out of our apartment and make my way down to the street, I reach in the pocket of my coat and pull out a knitted hat to stave off some of the coolness of the Sunday air.

Leaving our apartment on 121st Street, I quickly find myself walking along 125th. The broad "Main Street" of Harlem, stretches on for what looks like forever, the wide sidewalks filled with beautiful black people of every shade, all of them seemingly basking in the sun of the cool afternoon.

I walk past an African vendor selling books written by black authors. Several people walking near me stop and fan through the books. On the adjacent table is a collection of incense sticks and oils. Down a few feet, another vendor has bootlegged DVDs of movies still playing in the theaters laid out alongside CDs of singers or rappers with recent releases.

While the sidewalks are overflowing with people, I move peacefully through the crowd, uninterrupted in my thoughts.

I reach the Adam Clayton Powell Building and walk over next to the mural of three beautiful black women painted on the other side of the courtyard. The colors swirl in various pink, green, and lavender patterns, with an inset of the Apollo resting near a brown skinned queen, her head bowed, hands open to reveal a dancing figurine. I find a seat in what feels like the most solitary area of 125th and fix my gaze back toward the street, admiring the ocean of black people representing the various parts of the African Diaspora.

The masquerade ball is still very fresh in my thoughts, although it happened two days ago. I am extremely embarrassed about that whole situation.

Sitting at the table with Jean-Claude, Miles, and Melody, I must have gone through several Perfect-10s before I relaxed. I'm not really good with doing these social events, so the drinks were a necessary requirement. It might have been a recipe for disaster, in retrospect, though.

The morning conversations with Miles I've had these last few months have always had a kind of undertone to them. I sensed that he was just as interested in me as I was in him. Maybe it was something in his eyes or the softness of his tone toward me, but I felt that he was giving me signals that he was interested.

I can't help wondering what would have happened had Melody not shown up. I'm also very curious about what Miles is thinking right now, and if given the chance, would he have closed the deal.

———

JEAN-CLAUDE AND I DATED FOR FOUR YEARS before we married, and frankly, I didn't know if he would ever propose to me, given our spotted past.

Our courtship started out pretty traditionally with him coming to Jamaica, Queens, to visit me at my family's house. He would sit up and talk with my father and brothers for hours before we ever left to do anything ourselves.

As our relationship evolved, we got pretty hot and heavy, so I got on the pill. It had gotten to a point where we would have sex whenever and wherever we could squeeze in a hot, quick session. And more and more, I found myself enjoying it and even looking forward to it.

Then one day while sneaking a session in the back area of one of the city parks, we got into a really hot and heavy session, and Jean-Claude knelt down and lifted my legs over his shoulders, running his long tongue along my Southern lips. He tugged at them, and his mouth quickly enveloped me, pulling my clit around in the folds of my skin. His tongue was firm as he stroked me to the most mind-blowing orgasm I had ever experienced! Before that, I had had a few light orgasms when we had sex, but this was ridiculous! I literally blacked out for a few minutes. La petite morte is what Jean-Claude called it.

Once he got me wide open, I became a sex slave to him, and by the end of the first year of our relationship, we had graduated to involving others in our sex lives—well, actually just other women, because Jean-Claude didn't want me to be with any other guys. I loved him so much that I did whatever he wanted me to do, and it didn't really bother me, our bringing other beautiful women into our bedroom. A lot of them aimed to please me as much as they did him, so I got over the whole shock of seeing my boyfriend fucking other women.

After we had been together for a while, I realized that I could have a real future with him. Around that same time, Jean-Claude's first play was going into production. I wanted to tone down our sex lives to something a bit more traditional, at least keeping it between just the two of us. After all, if we were going to be together, I wanted him to make an honest woman of me, and that meant closing off our bed to others and focusing solely on me.

Jean-Claude agreed and went on to propose to me. However, it wasn't long after we had gotten married that I discovered that he had other women on the side. I take some of the blame for that, having let him have so much sex with other women throughout the majority of the time we dated. As long as he didn't flaunt the situations in my face, I felt I would be fine, and to a large extent, I've just learned to deal with it and know that as long as he practices safely and comes home to me each night, everything is fine.

I had been contemplating having a lover on the side for a while myself, and Miles is the first man I've actually entertained seducing. It took me at least a year to get up the nerve to even start "bumping into him" early in the morning before school would start. It was hardly an inventive idea, but I wasn't an expert at that kind of thing, unlike my husband.

I didn't go to the masquerade ball intending to make a move on him, but with the alcohol coursing through my system, I stepped up and ultimately put it all out there. I might've really messed up, though.

Now I don't know what to say to Miles. I feel like I might have caused him more problems with his own situation. I didn't really mean to get him in trouble with Melody. He just looked so sexy in that Egyptian get-up. I had to touch him, to taste him. And if he still wants to, I can give him a helluva lot more.

24

NOVEMBER 5, 2004

MILES THOMPSON

I f your life can change in a single day in New York, imagine what could happen in one crazy week.

Today I cancelled my afternoon lessons and decided to walk home so I could reflect over things. So much has been going on that I haven't really had a great deal of time to myself to sort things out. Since Ja came to stay with me last Sunday, I have been acting out one of the laws of physics like it was a personal mantra: A body in motion stays in motion.

On Monday I found myself subconsciously hoping to run into Teresa. I even showed up early at the school. I don't know exactly what I was hoping to accomplish, though. Over the course of the weekend I had gone through a rollercoaster ride of emotions, so maybe I just needed to bring some closure to the situation, something to let me know that we were still cool with each other. We see each other too much to be on awkward terms, and the last thing in the world I would need is for Diane Ford, our principal, to begin snooping around about the tension between a male and a female teacher on her faculty.

I sat in the teacher's lounge for nearly twenty minutes looking at *The New York Times*, hoping that she would come in for a morning cup of coffee. Throughout the day, I only saw glimpses of her from a distance, and I figured if she wanted to talk to me, then she knew where to find me.

Tuesday, however, was quite a different story. Coming in a little early, as was starting to become my habit, I ran into her preparing coffee in the faculty lounge.

"Teresa," I said softly, entering the room.

She turned around slowly to face me, smile in place, coffee mug extended toward me. "Hi, Miles."

We sat on the main sofa, facing each other. As I sipped the coffee, I looked at the steam and milky brown color inside of the mug, starting to feel a nervousness consume me. For a moment neither of us said a thing.

"How have you been?" I started.

"I've been wondering the same thing about you."

"Oh."

"Hey, Miles," Teresa said, looking directly into my eyes. "I'm really sorry about the other night. I didn't mean to get you in trouble with your date."

I noticed how she didn't say Melody's name, although I knew they had been introduced to each other on more than one occasion. Hearing Teresa refer to Melody as merely my "date" made me pause. Why did that bother me? Maybe it was because there was some truth in it. It wasn't like we had discussed a commitment. Often it felt as if it was merely understood, but now, according to Teresa's language, what was left unsaid was left undone.

I shifted on the sofa. Teresa placed her mug on the table. As she lifted her hand from the mug, I took in the scoop necked cashmere sweater she was wearing and how there was just enough cleavage visible for my imagination to run rampant. I looked at the smoothness of her skin and how the light danced off of her collarbone. For a moment, I thought of leaning over and running my tongue along the firmness of her neck.

She must have noticed that look in my eyes, because she eased up next to me, as I sat frozen. I could feel the soft exhalations of her breaths against my neck, and I remembered the light, fluttering kisses she had placed on me that previous Friday.

"Miles," she whispered, sending chills up my neck. "All you have to do is say the word."

My erection pushed at my pants so quickly that it ached from the pressure. I closed my eyes, feeling Teresa's hands relax onto my chest. I squirmed in my seat, my body lifting and falling slightly so that her hand would gradually fall down my chest and onto my lap. For a moment, all I could think about was feeling Teresa sliding down onto me, stroking me with all of that passion she seemed have trapped inside of her.

Teresa uncrossed her legs, turning toward me. As her leg slid over and between both of mine and she held onto my shirt to balance herself, I felt the incredible urge to fuck her senseless right then and there. She looked at me, her eyes half-open as if dizzy with lust, and I leaned in, planting my lips against her ready mouth.

As her tongue entered my mouth, dancing around in an almost violent way, her teeth tugged at my lips. I could feel the reckless way she kissed me, and I had a startling flashback to Melody's soft, tender kisses. The pang hit long and hard too, as I remembered not only how Melody kissed me, but how she touched me, held me, and made love to me.

Teresa continued kissing me as I finally felt myself beginning to resist. I mean, what in the world was I doing? It was clear that having sex with Teresa was not going to bring Melody back to me. It wasn't even going to take away that empty feeling I knew I would have later as I reflected over that morning. It's funny how sex starts to take on a different meaning the older you become.

"Teresa," I said, in between her kisses. "Teresa, please."

She continued kissing but slowed down as she noticed that I was no longer kissing her back. "What, Miles? What's wrong?"

"Teresa, I'm really attracted to you. I am. But this doesn't feel right."

"Why not?"

"Well, you have a husband."

Teresa scoffed. "You're not trying to marry me, are you?"

"Come on."

"What's really the problem?" She scooted over to the other end of the sofa. The breeze whipping up between us was cooler than I had expected.

"Teresa, I can't do this because I'm in love with someone else."

"Who? Melody?"

There it was: the name coming from Teresa's lips. Now we were two people talking to each other with no secrets between us.

"Yes. Melody." I shifted, adjusting my clothing. "I like you, but my heart is with someone else, and frankly, I'm at a point where I want to do things in my life that are right for me. If it was any other time or situation, I would be all over you like white on rice, but right now, I'm really trying to do the right thing."

She looked at me for a long moment and slowly nodded her head. I wanted so badly to know what was going on inside of her head. Had I led her on? Did she hate me now? Were we worse off than we were before that morning? I didn't know, and for the first time I actually felt a sense of freedom, not knowing what anyone else was going to do but knowing that I had been truthful to myself.

"It's OK," she said.

There seemed to be a lot left unsaid, but at the same time, I felt that she understood.

———

WHEN JA KENDRICK FIRST MOVED IN, HE GOT dealt a pretty devastating blow. I remember him calling one of his friends and getting off the phone angry. He left out of the apartment and went for a walk. "You OK?" I asked when he returned.

He didn't respond. He just sulked. I could tell that he wasn't just angry; he was hurt.

"I can't help you out unless you talk to me," I said.

He threw himself down on the couch and reluctantly looked up at me. "I don't know, Miles. Everything is just so fucked up."

I held on to my compassionate expression, although his language threw me for a loop. It always takes me aback when I hear young people use that kind of language.

"What's the problem?" I said, sitting down next to him.

"My boy Quent did a number on us. He did the record deal without us."

"Who is Quent? The heavy kid who was singing?"

"Yeah. That shady ass nigga."

"So how did you hear about all of this?"

"I just found out from my boy Yusef, the other guy in the group, that Quent did a deal with this producer dude we had been meeting with. That guy turned around and did the deal with Big Business."

I could see the crushed look on Ja Kendrick's face, but I knew what had happened had probably been for the better. I stood up and got us some sodas from the refrigerator. I handed him one. I knew that the conversation we were about to have would be a long one.

As we sat on the couch sipping our drinks, I explained in as clear language as I could how the music business worked. I told him about how the contracts were still outdated and amounted to share cropping relationships between the record company and the artist. I told him about the extremely high improbability of recouping the money the artist received as an advance against future album royalties. I told him about the additional costs that the record company charged against an already financially disadvantaged artist. I even told him specifically about how crippling the contract was that his friend Quent entered into.

"I don't understand. I thought the goal was to get a record deal. Hook or crook," he said, looking at me with confusion on his face. I knew that the conversation had to be miles over his head, given his age, but I pressed on, attempting to boil it all down to plain, easy-to-follow language.

"Remember what I said about the share cropping contracts? Well, a production deal is just flat out slavery."

I could see in his eyes that he wanted to understand, so I continued. "Because the royalties a record company already pays an artist amount to nickels, imagine paying that same general royalty to another individual who in turn gives only a few of those pennies to the artist."

"So what you're saying is that Terrell Bonds—the A&R guy—is going to be getting money that would normally go to Quent?"

"Yeah, but it's even more involved than that. Do

you remember what I told you about songwriting and how it's the key to making any real money in the music business?"

"Uh huh," he said nodding.

"Well, in a production deal like the one your friend is in—"

"He ain't my friend," Ja Kendrick interjected.

"Quent, I mean. In a deal like that, Terrell will probably end up writing all of the songs and producing all of the music. What that means is that all of the publishing and songwriting money will go directly to Terrell, as well as the production points for each track. In a nutshell, nearly all of the money that can be made from Quent's deal will go to Big Business and Terrell. And then there's the issue of him being a minor, but that's another story for a different day."

I could see his facial expression change, as if he was finding comfort in what I was saying. Suddenly he looked up and asked, "How did you learn so much about the music business?"

"The hard way, Ja. The hard way. If you've been around the business as long as I have, you kind of pick up on things. Truthfully, that's the only way to survive out there."

He looked at me and smiled. "Thanks. I mean, for everything."

"You're welcome," I responded.

I knew that was the first conversation of many that I would have with Ja Kendrick about music. With his talent, I realized that he probably needed to be more aware of the options he had that didn't include Big Business Records.

I ARRIVE AT MY APARTMENT BUILDING, MY MIND

still trickling with thoughts of the past week. Friday couldn't come soon enough.

The only major thing still nagging me is the fact that I can't seem to stop thinking about Melody. She's still not taking my phone calls, but I refuse to give up. I just don't believe in giving up if there's still a chance we can work things out.

When I reach the apartment, I find Ja Kendrick asleep on the couch. He looks as though he's getting some of the best sleep he's gotten in ages. Since he arrived, he's been doing a lot of sleeping. I can't say that I blame him, though. When you're tired, the best thing you can do is rest.

25

NOVEMBER 6, 2004

JA KENDRICK BROWN

Even though I know Quent probably signed a bum deal, I'm still pissed off with him. Since all of this stuff went down, he's changed his cell phone out, and he's avoided our phone calls. I guess it's safe to say that our group is officially dead. I don't really think that Yusef and I can hustle the trains without the main ingredient. It's just so foul the way everything went down. Now I'm totally assed-out on my funds. As each day passes, I get closer and closer to being absolutely broke. I need a job for real.

I haven't even tried to call Lei since we went out a week ago. I can't afford to take her out, and I feel kinda strange about the way everything went down with Big Business. What will she think of me since I didn't get signed and Quent did? I don't even know what I would say to her right now. I feel like trying to build on something with her at this point might be a bad move since I'm not gonna be in that loop anymore.

I've been beating the streets trying to find some kind of gig that would pay a decent wage, but I keep getting pushed away for whatever reason. I guess my age is the biggest excuse. There might be a lot of jobs out there, but there are even more people trying to get them. I'm just a fifteen year old with no connections, so I can't even get a shift over at the Popeye's on 125th Street, even if it was Sunday and church just let out. The best offer I got so far is to sweep out in front of one of the neighborhood bodegas for next to nothing. That ain't gonna cut it. I need cash, not coins.

I talked to Yusef today, and he's in the same boat I'm in—except he has his parents looking out for him. I told him if he heard about any jobs to let me know 'cause I'm starting to get pretty desperate. He said he's already started trying to scout out a few things and if he rolled upon something, then he'd holler.

SEVEN WHOLE DAYS. JUST LIKE THAT OLD TONI Braxton song. Seven whole days I've been staying at Miles's crib, and the funny thing is that I ain't been this relaxed in years. No stress at all—other than being broke as hell. I gotta admit that I been doing a lot of sleeping since I got up in this piece though. I didn't re-alize how tired I was. That couch is just so soft that every time I plop down, I'm out like the jheri curl.

I gotta admit that it's kinda weird, though. I mean, here I am crashing at this famous dude's crib, and he's looking out for me while I get my shit straight. Every morning when I wake up, I wanna thank him for giving me a place to sleep, eat, and shower. My mind's gotten a lot clearer too, and I've started back jotting chords down in my notebook.

Earlier in the week, while just looking around his spot, I noticed a picture of a kid on Miles's dresser. The kid looked enough like Miles for me to know he must've been his seed.

I stared at the picture for a minute and got a really strange feeling in my gut. Something just didn't sit right. I don't know if it was the way the picture was situated or the fact that it was the only picture in the apartment. Obviously there was something special about the kid, so I decided to ask Miles about it later that evening.

"Hey, Miles," I said, while we were sitting down to Chinese take-out. "Can I ask you a personal question?"

"Sure."

"Who's the kid in the picture on your dresser?"

He paused for a moment and said, "My son, Travis."

"Well, does he live in New York or is he back in Atlanta?"

He looked up at me. "My son is dead."

"Oh, man. I'm sorry. I didn't know."

"No, it's OK. You had no way of knowing."

I twisted my fork around in the lo-mein.

Miles took his time. "Travis was my only son. He was killed three years ago in Atlanta. He was—he was about your age."

I didn't really know what to say. I felt really bad for him.

"He was at a football game, walking around during half-time, when one of his friends got into an argument with a guy from another school. Things escalated, and the guy pulled a gun. He was intending to shoot my son's friend, but he hit my son instead. A single shot to the chest."

I shook my head. "I'm sorry," was all I could say. I know what it feels like to lose someone in your family, but I can't even imagine what it must be like to be a parent losing a kid.

"It's all right," Miles said.

We sat silent for a minute, not so much as a sound between us. Suddenly Miles shook his head and smiled as if he was remembering something.

"My son was an athlete. Boy, could he play some basketball! Could have led his team to State. But it didn't come easy for him at first. I remember this one time I went to see him, when he was still playing B-team, and the coach finally let him in the game because the team was so far ahead. The point guard passed him the ball, and I guess he was so nervous or something, and he shot the ball from about five feet outside the three-point line. That had to be the prettiest air ball I had ever seen."

We both started laughing, and Miles laughed so hard he started crying. At that moment I felt like I understood him just a little bit better.

"Have you ever been to Atlanta?" Miles asks, while we're chilling in the den watching TV.

"Nope."

"Would you be interested in going?"

"What do you mean?"

"I have to go down in a week for a house warming one of my friends is throwing. I can book both of us tickets, if you're interested."

I'm blown away at the offer and almost blurt out "hell yeah," but then I remember that's the city where his son died, so he might have some emotional baggage in behind that shit. Plus, I don't wanna be away from my sister for too long.

But on the other hand, I don't want him thinking I don't appreciate what he's doing for me. And he would be the one coming out of pocket.

I think I'll go. Who knows? It might be fun.

"How long would we be gone?" I ask.

"Just over the weekend."

"Well, cool. I could swing that. It would be cool checking out the ATL."

"Good. We'll get a flight out Friday evening and get back Sunday afternoon."

"Sounds like a plan."

"Yeah. I'll have to take you by and show you my old stomping grounds at Ellison-Wright College."

"That'll definitely work."

"Have you thought about what you want to do when you graduate?" he asks.

"I don't know. Something with music, I guess."

I ain't really thought about what I'd do after school. I was kinda hoping that this record deal would take off and blow us up.

"Well, there're a lot things out there that you could do. Look at me. I had no idea of what I would do after The Triumph's broke up. I wrote for a few other artists, but in the end, it felt like something was missing. I feel like teaching is where I'm supposed to be."

"I can tell you really dig teaching. You just don't seem like you get stressed out. I don't know if I could teach. I ain't never had no real music lesson in my life. Don't you have to have a degree or something?"

"It all depends," Miles says. "At the end of day, though, I would think that if you really felt passionately enough about your art, you'd want to learn as much as you could about it."

It all makes sense, but I don't know how all of that would work out. What if I find out that there's something that I totally don't know anything about and it winds up holding me back. I only know music from playing it. I don't know anything about music history or about any of the composers, except for what they wrote. Maybe I should consider studying music if I decide to go to college. Thinking about Miles going from being with The Triumphs to teaching music Uptown, I start wondering what the hell went down with his band. You don't just wind up in a place like this after you've been around the world.

"Miles, why did The Triumphs break up?"

He sighs. It's like he's wondering whether or not he's gonna give me a bullshit answer or break me off with the real 411. He looks at me and shrugs.

"It was a funny time," he starts. "My ex-wife and I had just had Travis, but the group was going through its own changes. Terry Jacobs, the lead singer, had been battling a drug problem for a while. Morgan Richmond, the drummer, had a problem keeping his snake in his pants. He spent more time in court on paternity suits than he did in the studio."

"Snake?" I say laughing.

"Well, you get what I'm saying," he laughs. "That's the gist of it though. When you have that much stuff going on in a group, sometimes it's good to just take some time off. We could never get back on track, though. I supported my family by writing for other artists and whatever publishing royalties I could get off of my work with The Triumphs."

"You think my group breaking up is a good thing?" I ask.

"I can't say. But it seems like you found out who your true friends are, so it can't be all bad."

I never thought about it like that. I know that Yusef is my boy. I think even Lei might be the real deal, but when it comes to Miles, I automatically know he's got my back.

WHEN I CALL MY SISTER, SHE ANSWERS ON THE second ring.

"Oh, baby brother, how you doin'?" she asks. She sounds different.

"I'm cool. What about you?"

"I'm OK. Just tired. What's the name of the guy you're staying with?"

"Miles. Miles Thompson."

"He seems like a good guy."

"He is."

Then I hear what sounds like Sherita crying into the phone.

"What's wrong?"

"Ja, it's just all so fucked up."

"Talk to me."

"Mama would hate me for forcing you out of the apartment. I mean, you're just a kid."

I can tell that she's in one of those twilight periods between being high and coming down. Her feelings get out of whack when she's coming down.

"I was gonna come and visit you. Are you gonna be around this afternoon?" I ask.

"Yeah. I'll be around. Kendrick, I'm sorry. I'm just so fucked up right now. I didn't mean to kick you out."

I wanna tell her that she didn't kick me out the apartment, but decide against it. I don't think she can remember what really happened last weekend anyway.

"It's OK," I say. "I'm good. I'll just drop through to see how you're doing in a few."

"Good," she says. "Don't forget. I'll be here. I ain't going nowhere."

I DON'T SEE A FOREST GREEN HUMMER PARKED ON the street, but I know that it could be parked anywhere. The weekend is always a hard time to find parking on this block, so I can't say for sure if Daryl's here or not.

I bounce upstairs to the apartment, and rather than just slide in my key, I knock on the door. The door opens, and I come face-to-face with the one dude I could have lived my whole fucking life without seeing again.

He's standing in the doorway in a red Coogi sweater with a huge platinum and diamond cross hanging around his neck. He looks at me like he could really give a shit.

"What the fuck do you want?" he asks.

"I just wanna see my sister."

"She's already blasted off. She ain't even gonna know who the hell you are."

"I still want to see her."

He shrugs his shoulders and says, "I don't give a fuck. I'm about to roll out anyway. Just don't be here when I get back."

As Daryl pushes past me and walks out the apartment, I walk back to the bedroom and knock on the door.

I knock again, and this time when she don't answer, I open the door. She's sprawled out on the bed in a tank top and a pair of oversized boxing shorts.

"Sherita," I say, trying not to scare her.

I walk up to her and put my hand on her arm. I shake her, and she moans but don't look up. She's lying on her side and a damn needle is hanging out her arm. I slide it out.

"Sherita," I say again. "It's me. Kendrick."

Her eyes crack open slightly, and she tries to focus them and keep them from rolling back in her head.

"Kendrick?"

"Yeah," I say, grabbing her hand. I squeeze it and feel her trying to squeeze back.

"S'fucked up. I need help."

"I know," I say. "We're gonna get you some help, but you gotta wanna stay clean."

"I know."

I rub her tangled-up hair like it's a sheet of silk. This is my sister lying here. Strung out. Wasting away. Sherita Lynette Brown. Mama wouldn't even be able to recognize her with the dark swelling under her eyes and all the tracks down her arm. While it ain't funny, my sister looks like a crack fiend from New Jack City.

I watch her drift off to sleep and remember my promise to do what I gotta do to move us up out of here. I made it out for the time being, but she's still here riding that horse. I feel guilty, like I should still be around taking care of her.

"I'm gonna get you out of here," I whisper in her ear. "I'm gonna work hard and save my money, and one day we'll live in a house out on Long Island or something. It'll have a fence, and we won't be near any of this drug shit that's around here. We'll have a yard, and we can grow vegetables and flowers and stuff. I'll have a piano that I can play, so we'll always have music in the house. And we'll be happy too, Sherita. We'll be like we were when we were little. And we won't hurt no more."

I sit on the edge of the bed for another half hour with my hand resting on Sherita's shoulder. Leaning over I grab a pen off the dresser. I realize she don't have Miles's info, so I jot it down and put it back on the dresser.

"Call me," I whisper in her ear. Then I kiss her cheek and leave.

NOVEMBER 12-13, 2004

MILES THOMPSON

"You OK?" I ask Ja, just as our flight touches down at Hartsfield-Jackson Airport just outside of Atlanta.

He looks at me, his face dazed and sleepy. He's taking everything extremely well, given that this is his first time on an airplane. When he finally went to sleep, not even the little bit of turbulence we experienced could have waken him.

"Yo, that was crazy," he says as we grab our luggage from baggage claim.

I had decided before we got here that I would just rent a car so I could show Ja more of the city. When we arrive to the car rental kiosk everything is in order, and within minutes, we are in our black mid-sized sedan cruising up Interstate 85, the night illuminated by the lights lining the highway and the downtown skyline glowing brightly ahead in the distance.

The radio is playing what sounds like a Jaco Pastorius song that's been sampled by a female R&B group called SWV. While they are singing about rain, I am admiring the clear night as we cruise down into the skyline, merging onto Interstate 75, headed toward our hotel in Marietta.

"Man, this highway is huge. What is it? Twelve lanes of traffic all the way across? Everyone must drive here."

"Yeah. They do have a train and bus system here called MARTA, but most people drive."

"Everything is so spread out."

"You know what MARTA means?"

"Nah."

"Moving Africans Rapidly Through Atlanta."

"You crazy!" He laughs.

"Tomorrow I'll show you where I went to school."

"Have we passed it already?"

"Yeah, it's back on I-20 West."

"OK."

We arrive at our hotel and check in. Tomorrow is going to be a long day. I am beginning to have a strange feeling that I will be confronting most of what I left behind when I moved to New York.

THE CAMPUS OF ELLISON-WRIGHT COLLEGE IS small and takes up roughly two blocks in the West End portion of Southwest Atlanta. The student body has always been just shy of three thousand students, which is one of the reasons I decided to come here when I graduated from high school in Tupelo, Mississippi. The buildings look largely unchanged, save a fresh coating of paint here and there. Once we reach the heart of the campus, I notice that there is a new building named after the college's most famous former president, Dr. Sabin Moore. I quickly point this out to Ja and he nods.

"Were you in the marching band while you were here?" he asks.

"No. I wish I had done it at least one year, but back

then it was a major commitment of time. I was trying to get The Triumphs off the ground and spend some time with the ladies."

Ja smiles. "So you were a playa then?"

"Not really. I wasn't really out there too bad, at least not like some of my friends. My roommate from freshman year had a different girl every weekend. Every time I asked him what was up with that he told me that the ratio of women to men was so off that he felt he had to help assure that every woman had at least a taste of a man before they graduated."

"That's crazy. And women fell for that?"

"Not all of them, but enough of them. That guy believed in playing the odds. He would walk up to a woman and ask her if she wanted to get down, and out of ten women, nine of them would slap him."

"What about the tenth woman?"

I smile. "That's the one who would get with him."

"One out of ten. When you think about it," Ja says, "those odds ain't all that bad."

"I would say that they're acceptable—if that's your thing."

We take a seat on one of the benches surrounding the main square of the campus.

"So you majored in music here?" he asks.

"Yep. There's a really good music department here if you decide you want to come down this way for college."

"Really? I ain't never really thought about leaving New York any time soon. You know, with my sister and all."

"I understand, but what you have to realize is that you have to live your life and let your sister live hers. Getting exposure to different places and different people is not a bad thing, you know."

"I'm not leaving my sister."

"I didn't mean anything about your sister," I say. "I guess that came out wrong."

"Naw, it's cool. I'm just saying that my sister really needs me right now, and I can't afford to pick up and come down here to go to school. Don't get me wrong though, the ATL is fire and whatnot. Ellison-Wright is definitely off the chains. I'm glad you brought me down here to peep all of this out."

"Well, I'm glad you decided to come."

As we sit gazing out at the trees painted with the Greek letters of different fraternities and sororities, Ja turns to me and asks, "You wanted your son to go to school where you went to school, didn't you?"

"I would have been happy with him going wherever he wanted to go."

"But you wouldn't have been mad if he wanted to go to Ellison-Wright."

"Of course not."

"You wanted him to be a musician, too?"

I drop my head and ponder the comment. Looking up, I catch a glimpse of two young ladies walking across the campus in purple sweatshirts and toboggans.

"Maybe. He never really seemed that into music. He was a basketball player."

"I think everybody loves music," Ja says, "but studying it is a whole other thing."

While the temperature here in Atlanta is cool, the breeze is not nearly as deadly as the hawk in New York. I close my eyes, feeling the wind blow lightly across my face like a lover's caress. Suddenly my mind drifts to Melody and her sweet face, her soft lips dancing across my mouth as she holds me tightly in her curvaceous embrace. The feeling of missing Melody melts into the feeling from missing my son, and my insides begin to feel hollow, empty.

"Yo, you a'ight?" Ja asks.

His words snap me out of my daze, and I look over at him. I'm not empty, I remind myself. The young man sitting next to me is counting on me to support him, and that's enough to let me know that I'm not alone in this world.

"I'm good. We should probably get ready to head on back to Marietta for the house warming."

RICHARD HARDIMAN'S HOUSE IS BURIED DEEP within a new subdivision, and the houses are so close together that you couldn't pitch a stone without hitting a house pointblank. Cars are lined all along both sides of the streets, so we park about a block away.

"Richard was my best friend from college," I tell Ja, realizing that I had never really told him anything about our host.

"Man, his house is huge! A house like that would cost like a million dollars or something in Queens."

"The real estate market is very different down here."

"About how much would a house in this neighborhood run?"

"I don't really know," I say. "But I'm guessing not more than $300,000."

Ja's eyes light up. "I might be able to swing that one day."

"Oh, you will be able to swing that. I have faith in you."

We approach the house, which is much larger than it looked from where we parked. Balloons are tied around brick posts that sit on either side of the driveway. Music is playing from the back side of the house, where I presume the patio is. I can faintly detect what sounds like Cameo's "Word Up." The smell of the grill

firing up hotdogs and chicken is like a finger beckoning us into the house.

"Miles Thompson!" Richard says, as I walk through
the door.

He pulls me into one of his ironclad bear hugs.

"How's it going?" I ask, regaining my wind.

"Blessed and highly favored, man." He looks
around me and spots Ja. "This must be the prodigy you
were talking about."

Earlier in the week I called to let Richard know
that Ja was staying with me and that I wouldn't be traveling alone.

"Yes," I say chuckling. "This is Ja Kendrick Brown."

Ja extends his hand to shake Richard's.

"Ja Kendrick, is this your first time coming to Atlanta?" Richard asks.

"Yes, sir."

"Well, welcome. It's a pleasure to meet you. I'm
Richard. Feel free to make yourself at home."

Turning back to me, Richard says, "Let me show
you guys around the house."

We walk through the spacious living room and
around the kitchen area, and I notice that Richard's
wife, Erica, has been busy decorating. Beautiful African-
American art prints of Jacob Lawrence, Romare Bear-
den, and Ernie Barnes are framed all along the walls.

Just as we make our way through the kitchen,
Richard leads us into the den/entertainment room
where there are a number of people lounging on a huge
black leather "L" shaped couch, children spread out on
the floor.

"Hey, everyone. This is Miles, and this is Ja
Kendrick," Richard says, introducing us to the group.

A smattering of hellos comes from the group as
they turn their heads momentarily from the 62-inch

flat screen television that's showing the movie *Coming to America*. I do a half-wave of my hand and Ja nods his head at them in acknowledgement.

Richard points to the back door where the patio is. "We'll make that the last stop. We got chicken, steaks, hotdogs, ribs, and all that good stuff smoking on the grill with my special barbecue sauce."

For a moment I lose myself in the memories of Richard's famous barbecue sauce. I remember I caught him whipping up a batch one time. I saw him putting in honey, brown sugar, hot sauce, and a drop of lemon juice before he caught me and forced me out of the kitchen. To this day he works to religiously protect his concoction like it's the secret formula to Coca-Cola or the KFC original seasoning.

Climbing the stairs, there are various family pictures. Richard's son, Alex, and his daughter, Jessica, are featured as we reach the top of the stairs. We walk around the second floor checking out the beauty of the interior decorating and the size of the rooms, and I begin to remember the dream I had about the baby grand piano in Travis's room. When we look into Alex's room, I realize that Alex has all of the things a seven-year-old child would ever want. I notice Ja inspecting the room. I can't imagine what's running through his mind as he looks at all of the toys and posters on the walls. I thought that I had spoiled Travis when he was little, but from looking at this room, I don't feel like I even came close.

As we head back down stairs, I catch a glimpse of the side of a woman's face as she walks around the bottom of the stairs. It's Bettina. And she's with some dude. I stop in the middle of the stairwell and lean back against Richard, who is standing directly behind me.

"Rich," I whisper. "You didn't tell me that you were inviting Bettina plus one."

"I didn't even know she was coming until Erica told me last night."

"Whatever you say, man."

We work our way down the stairs and toward the patio. Before we get within an arms-length of the back door, I hear my name in a tone that is all too familiar.

"Miles?" Bettina says, more as statement, although it has the inflection of a question.

I turn around and come face-to-face with her. I half-expect to feel some mild pang of longing when I look at her, but I don't. She looks somewhat the same, but she has changed some since our divorce, which was shortly after Travis's death. Her hair is no longer short. Braids cascade down her back in fine rows. Her face is glowing and she seems to have put on a few pounds. She looks happy.

"Bettina, I didn't see you," I lie.

"Well, I just got here." She turns away from me for a moment and pulls a rather stout, short, light complexioned man into view. It's the same guy I just saw her with. He is almost the same height as she, maybe a little taller. "I want you to meet somebody. Andre this is Miles Thompson, my ex-husband. Miles, this is Andre Shelton, my fiancé."

I shake Andre's hand firmly, attempting to ignore what has to have been one of the most awkward introductions that I've ever heard.

"Nice to meet you," Andre says after a moment of silence. And to make the situation even more awkward, he adds, "I'm a fan of your music."

"Thanks," I respond, not really sure of what to make of the compliment.

"Oh, Bettina, Andre, this is my young friend Ja Kendrick Brown."

Ja steps forward and Bettina looks at me wondering who the hell this fifteen-year-old kid is standing next to me.

"Ja Kendrick is one of my students, and I brought him down here to see Atlanta," I offer, although I feel in some ways my comment is unnecessary.

Ja steps forward and shakes their hands.

"So, Ja Kendrick," Bettina starts. "What instrument do you play?"

"Piano, ma'am."

"Well, you have the perfect teacher."

I move toward the patio door. "We were just about to grab something to eat."

"OK," Bettina says. "I'm going to find Erica and see if she can show us around the house."

I am relieved to get away from Bettina and Andre as Ja and I step out onto the wooden deck.

The view from the back of the house would be breathtaking if not for the immediacy of the other houses which seem to be intruding on Richard's backyard. It's as if the developers of this subdivision were trying to squeeze in as many prefabricated houses as they could.

Ja walks over to get a plate, and I step back inside to get a beer from the refrigerator since the cooler is empty. I enter the kitchen just as Bettina is coming down the stairs. She spots me as I open the refrigerator door and walks up to me.

"I have to talk to you for a minute," she says.

I grab a Heineken from the refrigerator and twist off the cap.

"Sure."

"I know we haven't seen each other in a while, and I know seeing me here with Andre is a bit of a shock."

"No, I'm fine."

"Miles, I know you better than that. I know that it's probably still a little strange—this whole thing."

"Well, maybe. Just a little. Especially with you knowing that I would probably be here."

"How do you think I feel seeing you show up with a kid that looks a lot like our son?"

I exhale slowly, and as I open my mouth to speak, she stops me.

"I'm sorry," she says. "I didn't really mean that. I know you're probably doing a lot to help that kid. You always had a good heart. It's just—it's just seeing you again and seeing the way that kid looks at you and re-membering how you were with Travis is really something."

"Ja Kendrick is going through some problems with his family right now, and he's staying with me until those things get sorted out."

She nods. "You OK though?"

"I'm good. I can't complain. Life could be better; life could be worse."

She reaches in the refrigerator and grabs a beer.

"You drink beer now?" I ask.

"Everyone changes," she responds, laughing.

As she takes a sip of her beer, she leans in close to me and says, "I have something to give to you. I fig-ured that you would want it."

Curious, I look at her, waiting for her to give me whatever it is.

Suddenly Andre descends on us like a jealous little dog that wants to compete for his master's attention. He pretends to not be listening to our conversation as he opens the refrigerator to pull out a beer.

Bettina pulls what looks like a CD jewel case from her purse. It looks like a Big Boze album. As I look at the CD, I realize that this is a single for the song that Big Boze sampled from "Tonight is Forever."

"I found this in Travis's room. The CD was actually in his portable CD player."

She hands me the CD, and I look at it. This is the CD I thought my son never got a chance to hear. I look away—to keep my composure.

"He was proud of you," Bettina says. "He was always proud of you."

"Thank you," I whisper, my voice weakening.

Travis was proud of me. My mind wrestles to comprehend this idea. I had always assumed he didn't care about my music. How good it feels to be wrong!

As Bettina and Andre walk away, I step back onto the patio where I find Ja seated in a lawn chair nursing a stack of barbecue ribs. I smile as I slide the CD into the pocket on the inside of my jacket.

27

NOVEMBER 13, 2004

BETTINA THOMPSON

Seeing Miles brings back a lot of memories, some good, some bad.

I still remember when we first met. He had just graduated from Ellison-Wright and was in the middle of his first tour when The Triumphs stopped in Birmingham, Alabama. I had just finished at Stillman College over in Tuscaloosa and had moved to Birmingham to look for a job.

At the time, I was crashing with Victoria Station, one of my girlfriends who had finished the year before me. I had been on her couch for about three weeks getting pretty depressed about the fact that I hadn't received so much as a callback on any of the interviews I had gone out on. She suggested we just bite the bullet and get tickets to see The Triumphs when they came through town. She figured that would lift my spirits. They were in heavy rotation on the radio, so by the time they made it to Birmingham, they were a pretty hot ticket. I believe they opened for The Commodores or something like that.

I don't even really remember the details of the concert, although I remember being so excited that I danced and screamed most of the night. When Victoria told me that she had run into a friend who could get us backstage passes after the show, I felt like things were finally looking up for me.

I think Miles took a liking to me immediately, and he apparently charmed me enough to come over to the hotel they were staying in. That first night all we did was talk and kiss a little. He invited me to come to the show the following evening because he wanted to see me again before they left for the next city, so I went. That night we did a lot more than kiss.

When he left Birmingham, I reconciled myself to the fact that I would probably never see him again. I knew I was playing the role of the groupie to begin with, so I wouldn't have taken it personally. He surprised me though when he called a week later wanting to fly me out to Chicago to stay with him for two nights while they were there touring.

We continued to see each other, but I was afraid to fall for him because I didn't know if it was all just a fling to him.

Then my period didn't come.

Shortly after that, my breasts got really tender and I would have problems keeping food down throughout the day. I waited several weeks before I broke down and went to see the doctor. I was told that I was nearly five weeks into my pregnancy.

I didn't know how Miles would take it, but I knew I had to have the baby because in my family abortion is not an option.

I waited patiently for him to call me from one of the cities on the tour, and for a while, he didn't call, and that scared me. Just when I was beginning to resign myself to the fact that I would never hear from him again, he called me from Philadelphia. I told him that I needed to see him, so he flew me up for a few days.

When I told him that I was pregnant and that the baby was his, I didn't know how he would react.

"Are you sure? I mean, have you gotten a second opinion or anything?" he asked.

"I'm positive I'm pregnant. The doctor has confirmed it, and dammit, I'm starting to put on a little weight."

"Damn," he said, sitting on the hotel bed. "And you're sure you want to have it? You know, I know this guy who knows this guy…"

"Miles!" I shouted. "This is our baby! And I'm going to have it with or without you!"

He sat on the bed with his head in his hands for what seemed like hours. Finally, he stood up and walked over to me. He hugged me.

"I'm sorry," he said. "I didn't mean to upset you, but this is all kind of heavy, you know."

I nodded. I was afraid as I stood there. I had no idea of whether or not this man would want to be involved with the baby.

"Well, if we're going to have this baby, then we should probably provide a stable environment for him or her," Miles said.

I looked up at him. "Miles, what are you saying?"

He looked around the room as if he were putting his thoughts together. "I guess what I'm saying is that we should get married and do this the right way."

I was floored. "Are you sure you want to get married? Do you even love me?"

He lifted my face to his and planted a soft kiss on my lips. "I do love you, Tina."

We married a month before Travis was born.

OUR MARRIAGE WAS NEVER PERFECT, AS I SUSPECT

no one's marriage ever is. Ours just lacked passion. I can't argue that Miles was a wonderful father to Travis, but it takes a lot more than being a father to your son for a family to work. You also have to be a husband to your wife.

After Travis passed away, I guess we lost the glue that we needed to keep our marriage together. We divorced quietly, citing irreconcilable differences several months later.

Since then, I've moved on with my life, and now I'm looking forward to starting a new life with Andre, my fiancé.

Although I talk to Miles occasionally by phone, I didn't expect that we would ever really cross paths again. Then one day while going through some of the things I had in storage, I found Travis's Discman CD player. I decided to play it, and I was shocked beyond belief when I heard what sounded like Miles's music playing in the background while a guy with a heavy voice rapped over it. I immediately thought that Miles should have the CD, should I ever see him again.

Then Erica Hardiman told me about the housewarming. I figured that Miles might be there because of how close he and Richard are, and plus, it would be a chance for Andre and Miles to meet.

Now that I have seen Miles and given him the CD, I wonder about him. I know the move to New York was designed to help him start over, but I just hope that he isn't running from himself in the process.

I also don't know what to make of that kid he brought with him. I know he misses Travis, but I hope that he's careful to not try to make this kid into the son that he's already lost.

28

NOVEMBER 15, 2004

JA KENDRICK BROWN

The ATL was crazy. At first I didn't know what to make of it. It's just so spread out, and there're so many trees! Everyone is pushing some kind of fancy whip down there—even at the colleges.

It was weird as hell seeing all of these cats just a few years older than me riding around in Benzes and BMWs. All those kids look like they had money. If it weren't for the few students I saw walking around who I knew were New York niggas, I wouldn't have thought I could ever fit in down there.

But all them bougie folks though? It just takes some getting used to, I guess. Me coming from Uptown, I'm used to everyone dressing the same way, taking public transportation and all. In the ATL, black folks live good! They dress good and push hot whips. It's a lot to take in if you're not from down there.

The campus was cool though. Ellison-Wright seems like it's pretty tight. Plus, niggas in New York know and respect that school.

Since I got back to Harlem, I been thinking that I should give some thought to applying there for college.

I just gotta make sure I get my sister up and running by then.

I STEP OFF THE 9 TRAIN AT 66TH AND BROADWAY and see Yusef standing in front of Tower Records, and I check my watch. It's 3:45 p.m. We're both a little early.

"Whassup, son?" Yusef asks, dapping me.

"You know me. Still Nigga-rachi wit mines. What 'bout you?"

"I'm good. Hey, let's walk."

We head west, and I realize Yusef must've come with a plan about funds. Since I got back from the ATL, I been more motivated than ever to come up with something. I guess that's why I was relieved that Yusef wanted to get up today when we hollered on the phone yesterday.

"Yo, I got some info on a job, but I didn't want to risk talking with you about it on the phone," he says.

"What's up? I'm broke as a joke and my money is funny, so holla atcha boy."

"You know Philly Sims?"

I shake my head. "Nah, man."

"Philly's involved in a line of business I can't really discuss out in public, if you get my drift."

I nod.

"Anyway," he continues, "He's in the process of expanding his operation from Brooklyn into the Bronx. He has some businessmen up there already looking to help build the enterprise. The only problem is that he needs a few young guys to help get the product to his people in the Bronx. He wants to move product using just a few carriers."

"I can't do that. I don't want to get caught up in that kinda shit."

Yusef looks at me and nods. "I understand. I just wanted to run the whole thing by you since he's paying me $1,000 to make each trip. I figured you could come with me as a lookout or something, and I could give you half."

I start to open my mouth, but then I close it. $500 per trip? I could wind up making a hell of a lot more money doing this than I could hustling trains.

"I don't know."

"It's not like we're dealing it. And we definitely ain't making it. We're just taking it from one person to give to another. I made a run over the weekend. No problem. Easiest money I ever made."

"I don't know," I say again. "You ain't heard about any other jobs?"

"Nope. The economy ain't what it used to be. Other than what I just kicked at you, I ain't got nothing else."

"OK. Well, let me get back to you on that."

"A'ight. Just know shit'll be popping off again real soon, if you tryna get in on the ground floor."

"I got you."

———

By the time I get back to Miles's, I've pretty much decided that I ain't gonna bother with any of that drug shit. If Yusef wants to get into that stuff, that's on him. I've seen what that stuff can do to someone. Just look at my sister. Perfect example of a good person gone to waste. But I can't lie. $500 a pop is some shit you can't just ignore.

Miles is sitting up watching television.

"How's it going, Ja?"

"I'm good. What about you?"

"Oh, I'm fine. By the way, I ordered pizza. It should be here in a few."

"Cool."

I sit down on the couch next to Miles and look at the TV. I don't know what in the hell we're watching. Suddenly a fine ass girl walks across the screen that reminds me of Lei Morgan. It's not Lei though, but the damage is still done. Now she's on my mind, and I'm missing her. Maybe it was stupid to try to avoid her.

"Miles, I gotta ask you a question."

"Go ahead."

"Do you remember the girl I told you I met at the studio? Lei Morgan?"

"Yeah, I remember her. You haven't mentioned her in a while."

"I know. You also know that my group broke up and since then I ain't really had no way to get funds."

"No, I didn't know that, but go ahead with your story."

"Well, I just wanted to know if it would be smart for me to continue stepping to Lei, even if I'm broke."

"Ja," he responds, shaking his head. "A woman is not supposed to love you just because of what you have. If Lei likes you, it should be because of who you are, not what you have."

"But she's in the industry, and she's always around niggas who will do for her. I mean, Miles, this girl is fly. She could get anything she wants from any guy she wants. Why would she still wanna chill with me?"

"Like I said, if she likes you, then it has everything to do with who you are as a person and not what you can do for her."

In New York, I'm not convinced that that's the way it works, but I decide that I'll still give Miles's advice a try. I grab the cordless telephone and walk back into the bathroom for some privacy.

"Hello?"

"Hello, may I speak to Lei?"

"This is Lei. Who is this?"

"This is Ja."

"I thought you had dropped off the planet," she says playfully.

"A lot's been going on. I don't know if you heard about my group."

"No, I didn't. What happened?"

"They decided to just sign Quent, the guy who was the lead singer."

"So what about you and your other friend?"

"We're out the picture."

"That's foul," she says. "They could have at least signed you guys to a publishing deal or something."

"Yeah, well, that's the way it all went down."

"So are you OK? I mean, I know that had to be real messed up for you."

"I'm better. I've been spending some time with my mentor just developing my skills and all. I'm thinking about going to college now."

"That's great! I want to go to college one day when all of this music stuff wears off."

"Really?" I ask, surprised.

"Really. You can't always be this young forever. You have to have a back-up plan."

I smile. Maybe Miles is right about women after all. I push ahead.

"Would you want to get together again and hang out? I mean, since I'm not going to be on the label anymore?"

"I can't even believe you would think I'd be done with you just because of the way things went down with Big Business. Plus, I like to keep my professional life separate from my personal life. So, yes, I would like to go out with you again, Mr. Ja. Is that all right with you?"

"You crazy, girl." I chuckle a little. "That's definitely cool with me. Do you have anything that you'd like to do in particular?"

"I'm open to whatever. We could see a movie or something, go to the park, go out to eat, whatever."

"Cool," I say, but in the back of my mind I know I'll still need to get a hold of some ends. Maybe not a lot, but I still need to be strapped with something. Plus with me trying to get my sister out from under Daryl, I'll definitely need to get something going with my finances.

"Well, I'll be getting at you real soon so we can hook up," I say.

"OK. And Ja?"

"Yeah."

"Don't wait so long to call me next time."

"OK," I say, trying not to cheese. "Well, you be easy, Lei."

"You too, Ja."

I hang up the phone just as I hear the pizza man standing in the doorway with Miles. The smell is going to work on my stomach, but now my mind is at work trying to find one good reason not to call Yusef back about his offer.

29

NOVEMBER 15, 2004

MELODY LITHCOTT

I have played out the masquerade ball in my mind a million times, and while I hate that all of that had to happen, I know it's probably more likely than not that Miles had little, if anything, to do with what happened.

I accidentally ran into Teresa a few days ago, and I swear I almost knocked that bitch out. She begged me to listen to her as she told me all about how it wasn't Miles's fault at all, and that she was out of place because she was drunk or some shit like that. I couldn't believe that she was going out of her way to try to clean up the mess, but I let her. And I was glad that I did, because later, I started to really analyze why all of this has made me so stressed.

I just feel like I have played myself. I mean, here I am preparing to really put myself out there emotionally, only to run into this situation. I realize that it probably has less to do with Teresa pressing up on him and more to do with the fact that maybe I want a lot more than this man is capable of giving me at this point in his life. After all, he's still getting over the death of his son. It seems like it might have less to do with him and more to do with me.

Maybe I should call him and get this off of my chest. I don't know, though. I don't want to play myself again.

30

NOVEMBER 16, 2004

MILES THOMPSON

Enough is enough already. I have to get Melody back. This whole thing has gone entirely too far.

While the idea has been floating around in my head for a while now, I just figured out what I'm going to do to bring an end to this silence. Interestingly, I got the idea from Ja, although not directly.

While straightening up the den last night, I came across a notebook. Thumbing it open to see what was in it, I noticed that it was Ja's notebook and that it was filled with music. I had no idea that he could write music like this! All of the melodies were complicated, but they were all written out well on the staffs. I knew he could play, but this was just flat out ridiculous! He had taught himself to write music—which is a whole other thing.

When I confronted him about his abilities to write, he said, "I just write stuff down to get it out of my head. It's no big deal."

Lying here in my bedroom looking up at the ceiling, it occurs to me that I will write Melody a song. And if she refuses to take my call this time, I'll just sing it for her on her voicemail.

Man, I must be losing my mind.

BECAUSE I HAVEN'T WRITTEN A SONG IN YEARS, especially one that represented my feelings, I assumed the whole process would be awkward and slow. I was wrong.

Sitting here with Ja's keyboard on my lap and a few blank sheets of paper beside me, I have no shortage of ideas about Melody. Her smile. Her kiss. Her eyes. My hand begins to move feverishly, and I stop at each line to whistle a rhythmic tune.

Once I get to where I feel the chorus should go, I think of how I had never intended to fall in love again. I think of how wonderful Melody is and how finding her out of all of the people in New York City and Atlanta is more than a coincidence.

I imagine holding her in my arms until she dissolves into me.

I roll that idea around in my head for a while, and gradually a melody (no pun intended) evolves from the chords I play on the keyboard.

"Dissolve," I say aloud to myself before writing it down.

I imagine being inside of her, making love to her, our bodies completing each other like the pieces of a jigsaw puzzle.

"Dissolve," I repeat.

I think of her smile, her voice, her warmth, her beauty, and I realize at that moment that I want to be with her for as long as she'll have me. I realize that I love her, that I want to be with her, and to my surprise, I am not afraid of this feeling.

By nine o'clock my song is finished. I play it a few

times on the keyboard as I sing along, and then I pick up the phone.

Again, I tell myself that I must be crazy. I'm not some kid in high school trying to serenade his girlfriend. I am a grown ass man. I used to make a living doing this, but I guess none of that really does much in the way of calming down my nerves. After I do this, I will have no more ideas. This is my last attempt at trying to get things right with Melody.

I dial her number. The phone rings and rings, and before I know it, her voicemail is picking up.

"Hello, this is Melody. I'm not here, but you know what to do." BEEP.

"Hi, Melody," I say. "I really miss you, and I just want the chance to tell you how I feel about you."

I start to play the keyboard and sing:
No more silhouettes, fantasies I can't forget
Girl, tonight I must admit that I want you.
I'll sing your body like my favorite song,
Caress your body 'til the break of dawn
'cause all I want is to turn you on tonight.
Feeling your thighs wrapped around mine
I need you to be mine tonight
This tension's just too much for me
You've got me craving your relief
I loose it when you look at me tonight.
Dissolve. Dis—
BEEP.
The voicemail cuts me off.

I try to find comfort in the fact that I was able to get out the main verse of the song. My heart is still racing as I place the keyboard up against the wall in my room and stare at the cordless phone resting on my bed.

Immediately I start to have this sick feeling in my stomach that I shouldn't have done that. After all, that's the kind of thing that can easily be used in the future to embarrass the hell out of someone. Not that Melody's that kind of person, but when you're angry with someone, there's no telling what you'd do.

I walk over and turn off the light switch. As I lie down on my bed and look up into the blackness of my ceiling, I find myself drifting away into apathy as I find that spot on the wave of sleep rolling across my eyes.

I DON'T KNOW HOW LONG I'VE BEEN SLEEPING when the phone starts ringing. I answer it, slowly bringing it to my ear.

"Hello?"

"Hi, Miles."

It's Melody. I immediately sit up on the edge of my bed.

"Hey, how are you?" I ask, putting a little energy into my voice.

"Were you asleep?"

"Not really. Just catching a little nap."

"At eleven at night, that's usually considered sleep."

"Well, maybe just a little sleep then."

I begin to think that the song might have worked. I haven't talked to her in a few weeks, and I'm overjoyed at even hearing her voice. This is definitely the most conversation that I have gotten from her since the masquerade ball.

"Miles, I have a question for you."

"OK."

"Do you really love me?"

"Yes." I don't hesitate or stutter.

"How do you know?"

"I just do."

"Did you love me that night at that masquerade ball?"

Although I sense this is a trick question, I answer, "Yes."

She is quiet for a moment and then continues. "Since the last time we talked, I've been doing a lot of thinking. I remember I told you earlier that I would just like to get any time with you that you could spare. Well, I realize that was a lie. After being with you, I wanted more than just to be someone you fucked, someone you hung out with. I should have been more forthright about that."

I listen, not really sure of where this is going.

"And when I saw how accessible you were to another woman's advances, I just lost it."

"But—," I start.

"Hold on. Let me finish. I realized at that moment that I needed to step back and evaluate where all of this was going. Funny thing is that I ran into Teresa a few days ago while I was in SoHo. It took everything in me to keep from drawing back and whipping her ass.

"But then she told me that she had had too much to drink and had come on to you, that it was all on her. She apologized for everything and said that you had nothing to do with any of that. Truth be told, I was just too tired to be angry with her. I just listened. When I got back home, I thought about not only what she said, but also all of those messages you left for me. And then you left this song on my voicemail. I figured that I needed to break the silence with you. I guess we need to resolve all of this one way or the other."

"Melody, can I say something?" I ask.

"Go ahead."

"After my son passed away and Bettina and I got divorced, I didn't ever think that I would be able to open myself up to love again. But so much has happened in the last few months to make me realize that I have to move on past what's already happened to me. Falling in love with you is something that I didn't see coming, but it's something that I embrace. I'm comfortable saying that you're the only one I want to be with. I need you, Melody. I do."

At first it sounds like she's laughing at me, but I soon realize she's crying. I don't know what to say to her. I don't know if I've already said too much.

She breaks the silence, her voice tender and loving. "I love you. I love you. I love you."

I want to reach through the phone and hold her. I want to feel her tears against my chest, each droplet of emotion being absorbed into my flesh where it can be devoured by my heart.

"I love you, too."

"I want you to come over. Right now."

"OK," I respond, putting on my shoes and grabbing my coat.

As I hang up the phone, all I can think about is making love to her until we pass out.

31

NOVEMBER 17, 2004

JA KENDRICK BROWN

Miles rolls out TMA a few minutes after 4:30 p.m. with a huge grin on his face. I'd decided I would catch up with him so we could head back to the crib together.

"Yo, why you cheesing so big?" I ask.

"I just found out that one of my students, Otharius Graves, will be studying piano at the Sorbonne in France this summer on a grant that we just got approved. He's going to love it."

"That's really cool."

Miles looks at me like he wants to apologize. "You know, if you were a student at TMA, I could have gotten you in on that grant."

"Yo, I'm not stressing that. I'm too old to attend your school anyway. Remember?" I say laughing.

"Yeah. But with your level of skills, I'm sure they'd be all over themselves in the department of Music and Musicology over there."

"Maybe. Maybe not."

"Oh, please! You act as if you don't have a clue as to how talented you are," Miles says, patting me on the back as we walk down the sidewalk.

"So you recognize my skills?" I joke.

"Helen Keller could recognize your skills, Ja."

We laugh for a moment.

"You think if I decided I wanted to go to school down South that I could get a scholarship at Ellison-Wright?"

"It's definitely possible. Are you seriously thinking about it? If so, I can help out."

"Well, I'm just trying to keep my options open and all."

"That's a wonderful option," he says as we reach the corner. "You would love it."

"Yeah, I enjoyed it when we were down there. I could see myself possibly going back if everything works out."

Miles smiles, and I find myself smiling, too.

"You feel up for going down to the Village? I want to show you one of my favorite stores," he says.

"Cool," I respond and watch as Miles hails a cab.

THE STORE IS OVER IN GREENWICH VILLAGE, ON the west side of the City, a few blocks away from the legendary basketball courts on Fourth Street. I don't get around to this part of the City much because people are on some other shit down here. You'll see a dude with a purple Mohawk or some chick with her whole face pierced up. Even with me being from New York, I get blown away by some of the shit I see down there.

"You like hanging out down here?" I ask.

"Sure. Why do you ask?"

"These people look like Rocky Horror, man."

"Well, there're a lot of different flavors down here. I'll give you that, but in the end we're all pretty much the same."

"You must be crazy."

"No, really. You'll see what I mean in a minute."

We hook onto another street and walk through a small doorway into a small, funky little record store. It looks like Retro City up in here, but I see photos of people I like on the walls. I see a poster of Marvin Gaye sporting a red skully and some silver platform boots. He looks like he's ready to do some damage. Over on the side I recognize a Sphinx and Pyramid with the words "Earth Wind & Fire" up under it. Behind the old cash register I see a picture of Stevie Wonder. It's a painting with the words "Hotter Than July" written across it. I feel like I died and went to old school heaven.

I look over at Miles, and he's already combing through a stack of CDs in a bin. Next to Miles is a guy with a huge green tattoo across his face. He's browsing through some Donnie Hathaway. Over in another aisle, I see two women, one bald and tatted, the other with orange pigtails. They're holdin' hands, and one of them is holding up an Aretha Franklin album. Now I see what Miles is talking about. Regardless of how crazy these motherfuckers look, in the end, they're people just like Miles and me, people who dig soul music.

"Ja, come over here and take a look at this."

I walk over by Miles and he holds up a CD and hands it to me. I laugh as soon as I recognize who's in the picture. It's an album by The Triumphs where all of the guys are standing in tight black leather suits with Afros and cowboy hats.

"Damn, Miles!" I say laughing. "They got you looking crazy on here."

"Oh, come on. That was the style back then."

"Whatever, man. You look like one of the Village People."

"Oh, you got jokes."

"No, I got truth."

Just as I say that, the guy with the green face looks at Miles. "Excuse me. Are you Miles Thompson?" he asks.

"Yes."

"Oh, man. This is so cool. I'm a big fan of your music, man. Really great stuff."

"Thanks," Miles says. "I appreciate that."

As the guy with the green face walks away, I ask Miles how he feels about people just walking up on him and complimenting him like that.

"It feels good. They buy the music, so the least I could do is thank them when they speak to me."

"That's really cool."

We walk around the small store for a while, and when we get ready to leave, one of the guys working behind the counter, a tall guy with dreads, walks over to Miles and asks him to sign an old Triumph's poster so he can put it up on the store wall.

"You know, I'm in here a lot," Miles says.

"Really?" the guy says. "I'm usually in from opening until the early afternoon. Glad I stuck around today. I'm a really big fan. You guys wrote some really kick ass stuff back in the day."

"Thanks."

"You live in New York?"

"Yeah, I'm teaching music over in Harlem."

"That's great. This your son?" the owner asks, nodding in my direction.

"No. He's a good friend of mine. He's the future of music, so watch out for him."

The owner nods and looks at me again.

"Good to meet both of you," the guy says.

When we dip out, I think about that last exchange, and something don't sit right with me. Maybe I'm just tripping about the props Miles is dishing out since I'm so broke I can't even pay attention.

Yeah, that must be it.

———

ALTHOUGH THE SUN IS GOING DOWN, WE FOOT IT up to Sixth Avenue and then over to Times Square. While we walk, Miles tells me about growing up in Mississippi and how when he was little, he would stay with his grandmama over in a town called Maben during the summer. Miles says that she could put a hurting on some peach cobbler. When I ask about him getting her to ship some up this way, he tells me that she passed away a few years ago. She had lived to be ninety-nine-years-old!

As we walk up Broadway past 46th Street, the music hits me like a brick wall. Just up ahead of us is a crowd of people forming a circle around some street performers on the street corner under the Morgan Stanley building. As we get closer, I can see them better. There are three guitarists, a keyboardist, a drummer, a percussionist, and four female singers dressed in earthy headwraps. Miles and I stop and stand outside the circle listening to this incredible explosion of soul all out in the open.

"You know that song?" Miles asks, leaning over and talking directly into my ear over the music.

"I've heard it. I know it's been sampled a few times. I should know this song. I mean, I love this groove."

"This is 'Sun Goddess' by Ramsey Lewis and Earth Wind & Fire."

"That's what it's called? Would've never guessed that."

"It's one of my favorite songs."

"Yeah, it's great."

We stand there for nearly twenty minutes while the group jams the hell out of that song, everyone taking solos.

It is only after we start walking back to the Times Square Metro station that I realize just how much I miss performing for people.

———

WHILE WE ARE GOING DOWN THE ESCALATOR INTO the belly of the subway, it hits me that Miles must really enjoy riding the trains.

"Hey, Miles, do you like taking the train or something?"

"I never really thought about it. It might be a subconscious thing."

"What do you mean?"

"Rather than be a Black man trying to flag down a taxi cab, I find it just quicker and less of a hassle to just catch a train."

"These cabs been pulling a Danny Glover on you?"

"No, but I know it's always possible."

"I see you like those gypsy cabs too," I say.

"Well, it's a lot easier to catch them in Harlem."

"True."

As we walk around the corner to get to the tunnel leading to the ACE line, another group of people is standing in a wide circle around a street performer. A Hispanic man is dancing to salsa music with a stuffed female dummy strapped to him on his legs and arms, and each time he takes a step, the doll moves with him. As he grooves around, shaking his ass to the music coming from his boom box, the crowd cheers, takes pictures, and drops cash into his tip can. Only in New York, I guess.

When we finally catch our train, Miles leans over

and says, "I'm going to get you a brochure for Ellison-Wright."

I nod, as I think back to the guy at the record store asking Miles if I was his son. I guess I was hoping he would've said "yes."

Suddenly Ellison-Wright is the last thing on my mind.

32

NOVEMBER 18, 2004

MILES THOMPSON

When I was younger, back when I was a teenager, there would be times when I would be driving down the highway and get the feeling that everything was perfect in my life, and I would get this giddy feeling that would swell inside of me and make me start singing. Whenever I felt that way, I would just say that God was smiling on me at that moment. Well, I feel like God is smiling on me right now.

When I saw Melody the other night, I had forgotten just how good it felt to have her body wrapped around mine. I kissed her for hours, as I held her body close to me. We made love in these ridiculously eroticized cycles. It was as if, through our lovemaking, we were trying to rewind time and make everything one seamless flow of passion from Day One.

After my third orgasm (and whatever orgasm she was on—since she claims to have lost count), we took a nice, long hot candlelit bubble bath. As I poured hot, bubbly water down her shoulder blades, I told her about the trip to Atlanta and how well everything was going with Ja.

"I'm happy for you," she told me, as her fingers interlocked with mine and she draped my arm across her soap-covered breasts.

"You know, the whole experience was cathartic."

"I imagine it was. You haven't been back there since you moved away, have you?" she asked.

"No. But going back there was liberating, and being there with Ja helped me to pit my present against my past, and I can actually say that I am ready to totally move forward with everything in my life."

"That's wonderful," she said. "And what does that mean for you and me?"

"It means that I'm in it to win it. I love you, and if you'll have me, then I am completely and totally yours."

She leaned back against my chest and tilted her head up, kissing me deeply as the steam from our bath caused a droplet of sweat to run down my forehead into my eye.

Since that day everything has been amazing between us.

And when I think about what a bright spot Ja adds to my day, I'm just feeling incredible. I have to admit that I was wondering what it would be like taking care of a young man again. I even questioned exactly what I expected to gain by offering Ja my place to stay. I think, in the end, I just feel that helping him is what I'm supposed to do. He's a good kid, and I don't think that God would have put him in my path if I were not supposed to teach him something or learn something from him. Ja is proof that what I'm doing with my life now is really meaningful on some level.

Couple all of that with the fact that the grant to send one of our students to study at the Sorbonne went through, and I feel like I am buzzing on Cloud Nine. I was really nervous about the grant going through, but with all that's been going on in my life, I haven't taken much time to dwell on it. I'm very happy for Otharius though. Our young people need to know the world is much bigger than New York City.

When I walk into my apartment, I am surprised to see Ja standing in the den with a broomstick up to his mouth and an old cowboy hat on his head. "Tonight is Forever" is booming from my stereo, and he starts lip-synching when he sees me walk into the room. All I can do is laugh.

"Come on, Miles," he yells over the music, tossing me a bottle of water to use as a microphone.

"Man, this is crazy," I say, as I watch him doing that slow groove dance step that we used to practice for hours to perfect for our tours.

"Don't leave me hanging," he says. "I'm about to get to the good part."

"Don't kid yourself, Ja. They're all good parts."

I pick up the bottle of water and start lip-synching alongside him, and for the first time in years, I remember how good it feels to perform—even if it's just faking around in my own den.

As the instrumental breakdown starts, Ja places one hand on his cowboy hat and rocks back and forth in some imitation old school dance step.

"No, this is how it's supposed to go," I say, jumping out front with my water bottle and doing a little slide step with the full spin and finger-popping added for flare.

I am so lost in my dancing that I forget how silly the whole thing must look to a teenager. As I look back at Ja, I see him clapping.

"You can move pretty good for an old dude," he says.

I nod and brush away the sweat that's starting to form above my brow. I'm tired now, but I dare not make that comment in front of him. Sometimes you just have to let these youngsters know what time it is and represent one time for the old school. But I know I'll feel all of this in my lower back tomorrow morning.

"MILES, DO YOU HAVE ANY MUSIC CONTACTS UP here?" Ja asks, as we sit down to dinner. Tonight we're just eating some leftovers from the previous night.

"What kind of contacts are you looking for? You trying to get signed or something?"

"Oh, no. Nothing like that. I'm about to turn sixteen, and I was just trying to get a job doing anything in the music industry."

"Well, I know a few people I can introduce you to. It shouldn't be a problem getting you an internship or something over at the music publishing company I have my co-publishing deal through. I could put in a really good word for you, and maybe they can get you in there as a paid intern or something."

"That would be so cool."

"We could also look into having you audition with METRO so that you can become a licensed performer on the subways," I say.

"Really? You think that'll work now that I'm solo?"

"Sure. By the way, when is your birthday?"

"In January. On the tenth," he responds.

"Well, we'll have to do something special for your birthday."

"Really? What?"

"It'll be surprise. We'll get your sister over and do something really fun."

"My sister," he says, his spirits beginning to fall. "We gotta get her some help."

I nod. I know how sensitive Ja is about his sister, and if I were paying attention, I would have been more careful to not bring her up at the table. Since the can of worms is open, I offer to discuss the situation with him.

"Has she ever been in rehab before?"

"Nah. I couldn't get her to go."

"Well, we have to convince her that she needs to go or else the rehab might not do for her what it could potentially do for her."

"I know. I tried to tell her that when I saw her the last time. She's gotta want to help herself for it to work."

"Yep. You're right." I try to soften the mood. "Your sister will make the right choice in the end. I know she loves you, and she wants to help herself get back right."

"I hope you're right. I really wanna believe you."

I lower my head and take a bite of my food.

Ja's voice, soft, yet distinctive, pierces through the silence of the room. "I need to believe you. She's all I have left."

"No, she's not, Ja. You have me, too."

33

NOVEMBER 19, 2004

JA KENDRICK BROWN

I've been back and forth about this for a few days, and I've decided that I'll do one run with Yusef. Just one. That'll buy me a little time until something more legit turns up. The good thing is that I'll be sixteen soon, so I can go after some mainstream jobs then.

I told Miles that I would be hanging with Yusef this evening. I think he was really cool with it because he was trying to do something with his lady friend tonight anyway.

After I lace up my Tims and toss on my bubble goose down jacket, I dial Yusef's number.

"Yep, guy, I'm on my way."

YUSEF MEETS ME AT THE TRAIN STATION DOWN THE street from his crib.

"You good, son?" he asks.

"Yeah. You?"

"I'm a'ight. Philly had some dude drop off three packages this morning. Got 'em in my backpack. I was told the whole thing should take a few seconds when we get there."

"I hope so."

"I got your money in my pocket. I'll give it to you when we get back inside of my crib. Don't wanna be whipping that shit out around here."

"That's cool."

We hop on the train and don't say anything while we ride to Times Square, where we catch the S train over to Grand Central Station and wait for the 5 train. I glance down at my watch. It's a little after eight. I hear a train coming, but it's the 6 train.

"How's it been going over there with that dude from The Triumphs?"

"It's good. You know, he's been real cool."

"Man, I wish I had somebody rich taking care of my black ass."

"It's not like that," I say. "He's just looking out for a brotha for a minute."

Yusef looks up at me with an eyebrow arched. "Whatever you say, man."

"Yo, Yusef, how long've we known each other?"

"Shit. A couple of years. Why?"

"I just want to tell you some shit that I ain't never told you before. You my boy, so I feel like you ought to know."

"Oh, shit, son. You're gonna tell me you gay or something?"

"Come on, man. You know how I am about the ladies," I say. I get serious. "I'm just going through some shit at home with my sister right now."

"So that's why you staying with that dude?"

"Yeah."

He nods his head. "I feel you. You and your sister trying to work it out?"

"Something like that. She has—uh—a bit of a drug problem right now."

Yusef looks at me. He opens his mouth to speak but closes it. He glances at his backpack and looks back at me.

"Hey, man, I'm sorry. I didn't know."

"Nah, it's a'ight," I say.

"No it ain't. I wouldn't have got you up in this shit if I had known you was dealing with that shit at home."

"It's cool. I'm straight. If it's OK with you, I just want to do this one run, then I'm gonna go back to looking something legit."

"I understand," he says. " You know, you ain't got to roll with me if you don't want to. I mean, I understand. You can head back to the crib, and I'll just get at you tomorrow. I'll still give you your half of the money."

"I ain't gonna bail on you tonight. You my boy. We in this together."

"You sure?"

"Yeah," I say.

I can hear a train approaching. This time it's the 5 train.

Yusef looks at me. "You know, you're OK with me. I don't care what them other motherfuckers say about you."

I laugh as I pat him on the shoulder.

When the train stops, we get on, ready to get this whole thing over with.

"You heard from Quent?" I ask, while the train rocks back and forth.

"Nah, man. Fuck that nigga. If I see him, I'm gonna stomp him."

"You know, I ain't even mad at him no more."

"Where the fuck is this coming from?" Yusef asks, amused.

"I just been doing some thinking. I talked with Miles, and he told me the type of deal Quent signed was just jacked up anyway. Since then I've been thinking that I need to keep my options open. I'm thinking about going to college."

"College? That's what's up. I've been thinking the same thing. But I'm still gonna stomp Quent though. There's just principalities in this shit. I mean, Ja, you my boy, right?"

"Mos' def'."

"And you wouldn't stab your boy in the back, now would you?"

"Of course not."

"See, it's about respect. That's all."

"I see."

The train stops, and I look at Yusef.

"We get off a few stops down," he says.

"OK."

I rub my hands together. I didn't realize that they were even sweating. My stomach is doing all kinds of things, and I'm just counting the minutes until we get back on this train headed back to Yusef's crib in Brooklyn.

"You ever get up with that shorty from Deja Ice?" Yusef asks.

"You know that!"

"You cut that?"

"Man, I really like her. I'm trying to build something with her."

"So you ain't hit it yet?"

"All I'm saying is that she can put her finger in the

air 'cause she's the one! You don't cut 'the one' until the time is right."

"Ah, Ja is catching feelings."

"Who can blame me?" I say.

"I ain't mad atcha."

The train stops again. Yusef cranes his neck to see the sign on the platform.

"I think we're the next one," he says.

I sit back and move my fingers across my lap like I'm tickling the ivories. I do it sometimes when I start to get nervous.

"You know where you want to go to college?" he asks.

"I'm thinking about Ellison-Wright."

"That's down South, ain't it?"

"In the ATL. Miles took me down there last weekend. Yo, it was fire! A lot of really cool people down there."

"I'm thinking about City College, but I'll have to come down and holla at you on spring break or something."

"That'll work."

The train stops again, and we get off this time. I follow Yusef out the station and down the stairs to the street. When we reach the bottom, Yusef loops around the stairs and heads back into a dark area under the tracks.

"Hey, I'm gonna walk over there by that steel beam. That's where I'm supposed to meet this guy. You hang back off to the side. Just keep your eyes open for the Po-Po."

"OK."

I get situated and do a cursory look around. We're nearly covered by the shadows from the overpass, but everything looks clear.

I glance down at my watch. It's a little after nine.

I'm too ready for this transaction to go down because it's kinda creepy up under here. I'm Harlem born and bred, so I don't feel comfortable hanging out in the 'hood of another borough if I don't spend a lot of time there. I look over at Yusef, and I see a guy up ahead in the distance. He does a funky gesture with his hand and Yusef nods. This must be the guy.

The guy is bald and dark-skinned, sporting a brown leather jacket. He approaches Yusef slow and easy. When he gets in front of Yusef, I can barely see the exchange. I glance out the side of my eyes checking for 5-0. That's when I spot it. The forest green Hummer. It's parked on the corner, and I can barely make out the guy behind the steering wheel, but I know who it is. And I know that we're in a place that we definitely don't need to be.

I see Yusef zip up his backpack and start walking back towards me.

Then I hear a voice. "Wrong block, kid! Wrong motherfucking block!"

I hear the gun popping off, and I look up just in time to see the bald guy fall. I catch a glimpse of a skinny kid in a Yankees jacket firing his gun in my direction, and my instinct is to run as hard and as fast as I can.

"Yusef! Run!" I scream, as I take off down through the darkness. Everything is moving in slow motion, and my heart is pounding so hard I can't think. It feels like my calves are about to pop off my legs.

I hear several more shots fire, and then something knocks me forward. It feels like it's burning a whole through my body. I feel my feet come out from under me, and just as I land in the dust and gravel, everything goes black.

34

—————

NOVEMBER 19, 2004

MILES THOMPSON

I step out of the shower and wrap a towel around my waist. I can already sense that I will be running late for my evening with Melody. After drying, I brush my teeth while humming "Dissolve." Since the other night, I have completely turned myself over to love, and it feels amazing! We have seen each other every night this week, but because this is Friday, I get to spend a complete uninterrupted night being seduced by this beautiful queen of mine.

My clothes are spread out on the bed, and I spray a light mist of cologne around my neck and onto my wrists. I reach for the hound's-tooth slacks on my bed and put them on. My camel colored cashmere turtle-neck sweater is hanging in the fold of the accordion doors of my closet. When I walk toward the closet to get it, I see my caller ID flashing. I don't recognize the number, but whoever has been trying to call me from this number has called more than five times in the last five minutes.

I pick up the phone and dial back the number, waiting as it rings.

"Miles?" the voice says hysterically.

"Who is this?" I ask.

253

"Sherita, Kendrick's sister. Something's happened to my little brother."

She's speaking so fast that I can't keep up with what she's saying.

"You said something happened to Ja? But he's out with his friend in Brooklyn."

"Miles," she says pacing her words now. "My brother's been shot."

I feel myself falling back onto my bed. A sick feeling settles in the pit of my stomach as I glance over at Travis's picture on my dresser. *Lord, please don't do this to me again.*

"I've got to get to Mercy Hospital in the Bronx. They just called me a few minutes ago."

"I'm on my way to your place. We'll go together."

I hang up the phone and rush to get on my shoes and grab my coat. I grab my cell phone and call Melody, while trying to hail a gypsy cab. My mind is racing and my legs are weak as I step into the first vehicle that stops.

"Hello," Melody says, answering her phone.

"Baby, something's happened to Ja. He's been shot. I'm on my way to the hospital."

My eyes are glassing up, and my heart thunders in my chest. It feels like the cab is moving in slow motion.

"Can we go faster, please?" I yell at the driver.

I hold the phone to my ear, and I realize my hand is shaking.

"Baby, are you still there?" Melody says, her voice trembling.

I take a deep breath, trying to do whatever I can to calm myself. "I'm headed to get his sister and go on to the hospital from there."

"Do you want me to meet you at the hospital?"

"No, that's OK. We're headed to the Bronx. Just wait to hear back from me."

"Miles, I love you, and I'll be praying for Ja."

"Thank you, baby," I say. "I love you, too."

I close my phone and place it back in my jacket pocket. I wipe my eyes, but the street is still a blur when we pull up at Sherita's apartment. She is standing at the curb and hops into the cab, her face streaked in tears.

When she sits down next to me she collapses in my lap.

"No!" she screams. "No!"

I rub her back and try to calm her down. The cab driver looks at me through the rearview mirror.

"Drive faster, man!" I yell. "Someone's been shot, dammit!"

The cab flies down the street as if possessed. Within minutes, the cab pulls up in front of the hospital. I pay the driver as Sherita leaps from the cab. We run into the hospital and stop at the first kiosk we come to.

"I'm looking for Ja Kendrick Brown. We're family," I say to the attendant sitting behind the desk.

She punches at the keyboard of her computer, and in moments she tells us that, according to her records, Ja is still in the emergency room.

"Go to the third floor. There is a waiting room up there. Let them know you are family and are here about Ja Kendrick Brown, and they will get a doctor to speak with you as soon as possible."

As I hold Sherita steady while we walk through the corridor to the elevator, I begin to have flashbacks. The white walls and the smell of disinfectant remind me of when Bettina and I walked into Grady Memorial in Atlanta three years earlier. I will myself to be strong for Sherita, but my legs feel as if I am walking through water with leg weights. When we reach the elevator, Sherita presses the "up" button frantically.

"It's going to be OK," I tell her, but I'm just as afraid as she is.

I stare at the elevator and look at the lit numbers moving above the door. Why is this elevator going so damn slow?

I feel myself getting worked up again, so I pause and take another deep breathe, something one of my therapists recommended after Travis passed. While I breathe, I pray. I know it's been a while since I've been to church, but at this moment, the floodgate bursts open and I talk to God as if it is the last thing that I will ever do.

Save this young man, I pray. Spare him, please.

The elevator opens, and we step on. I press the button for the third floor, because I don't think I can take Sherita banging the buttons in here. She is still sobbing loudly, and I turn to face her.

"Sherita, we have to be strong for Ja Kendrick right now. We gotta hold it together. OK?"

She nods at me, her eyes helpless.

The elevator lets us off at the third floor, and I go over to the kiosk and tell the nurse that we're here to see about Ja Kendrick Brown. She tells me to have a seat in the Waiting Area.

"Can you tell me anything?" I ask, attempting to keep my voice calm.

"Well, sir, he's still in the ER. As soon as we know something, we will let you know. Are you family?"

"Yes," I respond.

"Well, if you don't mind, we need you to fill out a few forms for us."

"OK."

She hands me a stack of papers and a clipboard. I

turn to Sherita. "I'm going to need your help filling these out. OK?"

She nods.

We take a seat in the first empty chairs we come to, and Sherita and I work through each page as best we can.

"I wish someone would tell us something," Sherita says, resting her head in her hands.

"We should know something soon."

As I sit in the chair, I wonder what in the hell Ja was doing in the Bronx anyway. I realize that I don't have a clue as to what happened.

"Miles," Sherita says softly.

"If my brother survives, I'm getting my shit together first thing."

I look at her, unsure of what to say. "All right."

As we sit patiently waiting to hear from the doctor, a police officer walks over and stands directly in front of us.

"Excuse me, but are either of you the family of Ja Kendrick Brown."

"We both are," Sherita says.

"I have just a few questions for you."

"Officer, can this wait until after we hear from the doctor?" I ask.

"Well, actually, sir," the officer responds, "we have a suspect at large and any information that either of you could provide would be very helpful."

"What happened to my brother?" Sherita asks.

"Your brother was shot in what we have reason to believe was a drug deal gone bad. The other two young men at the scene were already deceased when we arrived. Your brother was still alive when he came in, I believe."

"Oh lord!" Sherita says, grabbing my hand.

"We have reason to believe that Ja Kendrick and

two others were attempting a transaction in a territory rumored to be controlled by a Daryl Tucker. One of our witnesses stated that two men fled the scene in a green Hummer."

Sherita collapses in her chair in a hysterical fit of crying.

"Come on, Sherita," I say, holding her in my arms. "You've got to hold it together. We're going to make it through this."

The police stands by patiently as Sherita composes herself.

"I have a few things I can tell you, officer," Sherita says, rising from her seat and walking over to the side to talk to the officer.

I lower my head onto my fists and look at the floor. I feel nauseated when I think about that hospital in Atlanta. When Bettina and I had arrived at Grady, we weren't there because our son was in the ER. We were there to identify his body.

As I sit in this chair, I try to put it all together, to make sense out of everything. What in the hell was Ja doing in the Bronx, and how did he get caught up in a drug deal gone bad? It just doesn't make sense. Why? Why would he jeopardize his future like this? It just doesn't make any sense.

I stare at the floor, my eyes involuntarily making patterns from the charcoal slashes decorating each of the off-white squares on the Waiting Area floor. I shake my head and wipe my eyes. It couldn't have been about money. Could it?

As I reflect over some of the conversations I had with Ja a few days ago, I get the feeling that I totally misjudged the situation. He had been talking about the fact that he needed money. He had talked about trying to get a job as soon as he turned sixteen. How could I have missed the signs?

My head falls more deeply into my hands. I could have prevented all of this by giving him some money to hold onto in the meantime. Now I'm sitting here allowing history to play itself out on me again.

For a moment I shake violently, angry with myself, frustrated that something this horrible could happen under my nose.

I should have been stricter on him or something. I should have opened a more honest dialogue with him about drugs, especially since we had just talked about Sherita.

The feeling turns my stomach so badly I have to stifle vomiting.

I could have prevented all of this, and I could have prevented Travis's death by simply insisting that he sit down to dinner. One second could have made all the difference in the world. If I just hugged him one last time before he walked out the door, maybe he would still be here. If I had read between the lines with Ja, he would be laughing and lip-synching around my living room right now, being a kid, a good kid.

I stare at the floor through glassy eyes. Then I look over at Sherita, who is now seated with the police officer. She seems to know a lot, and I want to ask her what she knows when she finishes up, but then it hits me that her boyfriend must in some way be involved in what happened to Ja.

I get so angry that for a moment I am just paralyzed. I have so many emotions running through my body that I feel as though I will explode. The human body just doesn't seem like it was designed to be stretched to this limit. I am reduced to thinking in prayers because I can't take it any more.

I don't even see the doctor walking toward me until he gets right up next to me.

"Hi, I'm Dr. Shedrick Connor. Are you here for Ja Kendrick Brown?" he asks.

"Yes," I respond, as I beckon Sherita over.

"Well, Ja Kendrick was shot once in the back with a nine millimeter handgun. He's currently in critical condition. We were able to control the bleeding, but we're going to need to see if we can retrieve the bullet fragment to prevent irreparable damage. We're prepping him right now for the OR."

I nod and look at Sherita. Tears are beginning to well up in her eyes again.

"We'll be right here when you know something, doctor," I say.

He walks away quickly, and I'm left with the feeling of falling.

As I sit next to Sherita, I find that I don't have any words. She sits beside me silently, wrestling with her own feelings.

I look around the room, and just outside the windows is blackness punctuated with only the light of street lamps. Somewhere out there in that blackness two men are running around, hiding from the law.

Frustrated, I close my eyes and feel myself starting to drift off.

I wake to Dr. Connor standing over me, Sherita standing beside me.

"Ja Kendrick has been stabilized. We were able to remove the bullet, and he's been moved to ICU. I have to tell you though, his heart stopped for about a minute during the operation. We don't know if there will be any brain damage or the extent of nerve damage he might have gotten from the bullet moving through his system. We should know in the next day or so what his condition will be. He's asleep, but you're welcome to go by his room for a moment and see him if you'd like."

I rise to my feet and shake the doctor's hand. "Thank you."

WHEN I STEP INTO THE HOSPITAL ROOM AND SEE Ja Kendrick lying unconscious on his bed, I have to pause to gather myself. Beyond the tubes and IV drip, I see the monitor indicating his heart pattern. He is breathing—on his own.

Sherita walks into the room and kneels down on the floor next to the bed. She places a hand delicately on Ja's.

"I'm so sorry, Kendrick. I'm so sorry. Please forgive me." She sobs as she leans against the bed.

I step outside the room and lean against the wall next to the door. I lift my head and wipe the corners of my eyes.

I turn back and look at Ja lying in his hospital bed. He's not out of the woods yet. Anything could happen tonight. And if he makes it through the night, there's a chance he might come out of this paralyzed or possibly a vegetable. He might not ever play the piano again. He might never be the same.

I'm thankful he's alive at this exact moment, but I know that everything is entirely outside the hands of the doctors now.

I walk back into the room and place my hand on Sherita's shoulder. We pray over Ja, and I call the nurse to give Sherita pills so that she can relax and go to sleep for a while.

Standing over Ja's bed, I watch his chest rise and fall with each labored breath. I want so badly to go turn back the hands of time. It seems like the cruelest act of nature for this situation to happen to me twice. There is only so much a man's heart can take.

I take Ja Kendrick's hand and know that there is only one thing I can do at this point: leave it all in the hands of God.

35

NOVEMBER 21, 2004

MILES THOMPSON

My back feels as if I have been sleeping on an uneven pile of bricks. I lean forward until I hear it pop in several places. As I push forward and stand up, I see Sherita seated over by the bed, her head resting near Ja. He still hasn't come to, and with each passing day, I feel more and more afraid of the ultimate diagnosis.

The doctor informed us that it was OK for us to talk to him, though, and Sherita and I have alternated back and forth between our own private talks to Ja. Sherita has been really fighting to be here with her brother. I can look in her eyes and see that it's killing her to not go and get that next fix. She's holding out, but I can't tell for how long. She really needs some help if she's going to be able to look after Ja when he comes to.

I find that I am often watching the heart monitor, observing his chest rise and fall. Just seeing him breathing is really enough for me at this point.

Sherita hears me moving around and wakes up. She smacks her lips. "I'm thirsty. I'm gonna get something to drink. You want anything?"

"No thanks," I say. I take a seat in her chair after she leaves the room.

I look down at Ja and start talking about whatever crosses my mind.

"You know, there was a time when I thought I would never get over Travis. It was just too hard. I mean, burying your son is not something that any parent should have to do. I mean, what can you do? Your life just seems so empty and worthless, like the best of what it is you had to offer has been scattered to the four corners of the wind." I reach out and pat Ja's hand. "But it's funny how life works out. My coming to New York to teach. As my grandma would say, 'Who would've ever thunk it?' I swore up and down that I would never teach. The older I get, though, the more I realize that we are all constantly evolving. Look at you. You have evolved into a wonderful kid and one of the most talented musicians that I have ever known, and you did it all by the age of fifteen. You've accomplished so much in the few years you've been on this planet.

I find it hard to imagine what my life would be like if I hadn't gotten to know you. You've helped to remind me that I still matter, that God can grant second chances in life. I know that you're going to get better. I also know that you are going to continue making beautiful music and touching the lives of everyone you meet. That's the way people with your spirit are. They continue to bless people with their talents."

I stand up and stretch my arms, attempting to stifle a yawn, and as I sit back down, I see Ja's eyelids flutter, as if he's trying to open them.

"Ja?"

He opens his eyes and quickly squints them because of the light coming through the blinds.

"Ja!"

His lips move slowly as he starts mouthing something.

I quickly buzz for the nurse, who comes in and begins checking on him.

As I stand back, I notice the faint trace of a smile spreading across his lips as he looks at me.

"You scared me," I say, as Sherita and I sit around Ja, who is now propped up on some pillows.

"I'm sorry for everything," he responds, his voice faint, a whisper of its normal volume.

"I'm just glad you're OK, little brother," Sherita says.

He nods. "Sherita, I need you to do something for both of us."

"Sure."

"I need you to get some help. You gotta get better."

She drops her head and looks away from us, embarrassed. "I know."

"I mean it. It's gotta stop. We gotta start being a family again."

This time she only nods.

I reach over, taking Sherita's hand. "We're going to support you. You're not alone."

Sherita nods and wipes her eyes with the back of her hand.

I look back at Ja. "I'm glad you're all right."

Ja smiles, as he wiggles his fingers. "I still got it, too."

"Yes. You still got it."

36

MARCH 1, 2005 (FOUR AND HALF MONTHS LATER)

SHERITA BROWN

After we found out Kendrick would be OK and got him back to Miles's, I decided to check myself into rehab. I was there for three months, and I swear I thought I was gonna die those first two weeks. It felt like my body was breaking down on me, and I would have given up and checked out except for the fact that I wanted to be clean this time. Not just for Kendrick, but for me.

While I was in rehab, Daryl got picked up by the police. The D.A. hit him with a stack of charges on everything from first degree murder to possession with intent. No bail either. Plus, it was his third strike.

In retrospect, I don't know how I let that man into my life and allowed him to take over. Now that I'm clean and have a clearer head, I realize that I just needed to be rescued by someone. And he was willing to rescue me.

He was a good guy at first, too. Real flashy, but sweet. He made me feel like a woman, like I mattered. And the pressure of trying to take care of my brother just led me to trying different things to take off the edge, and that just so happened to be what Daryl specialized in. Before I realized it, I was lost.

Now that I have all of that out of my life, I can move forward and be who I need to be. It's like I got this whole new lease on life. I'm gonna get it right this time. I just have to take it a day at a time.

I'VE BEEN SPENDING A LOT MORE TIME WITH Kendrick, but I told him to stay with Miles until he finished out the school year so that he could stay focused. He's even looking to apply to some summer program at a college down in Atlanta this summer.

I'm gonna miss him, although he'll only be gone for six weeks. But at least I have a new job to keep me busy in the meanwhile. I was hired a few weeks ago to do customer service for Nextel. Maybe if everything works out, I'll go back to school myself. Wouldn't that be something?

37

JUNE 4, 2005

EPILOGUE

When we pull up at the airport, I exhale.

"You OK?"

"I'm good."

"Don't worry. You'll love it."

I smile.

As we get out the cab, the driver pops the trunk. I pull out my suitcase and set it on the curb.

We step into the airport and walk over to the ticket counter for my flight.

"Next!" the Donny Osmond-looking dude calls out. I lift my bag and step up to the counter.

"Name?"

"Ja Kendrick Brown."

"Destination."

"Atlanta."

After checking my ID and bags, he hands me a boarding pass. I walk back over to the spot where Sherita and Miles are standing.

"How do you feel?" Sherita asks.

I look at her and smile. I like the "new and improved" Sherita. She looks so happy now, nothing like she looked before she cleaned up.

"I feel pretty good."

"Ellison-Wright has no idea of what they're getting in you," Miles says patting me on my shoulder.

As I stand there looking at them, I start to choke up. I still can't believe I'm going to Atlanta for the summer. Part of me is really looking forward to seeing how I'll make it down South; the other part is sad to be leaving the only home I've ever known and the only real family I've got.

"Be good, little brother," Sherita says, hugging me hard and kissing me on the cheek. "Don't go down there and break too many hearts."

"You know I won't do that. I'm off the market. You know that," I joke. "Actually, I'm supposed to see Lei tomorrow night. Deja Ice is coming through the ATL to do a promo for their new album."

"I ain't mad atcha," she says with a smile, nudging my arm.

The thought of seeing Lei makes it a little easier to board the plane. Over the past few months, she and I wrote a couple of songs for her upcoming solo project. I even had to start my own publishing company through ASCAP (Angela's Boy Publishing). How cool is that?

Miles steps in front of me and looks directly into my eyes. "You're a good, kid," he says. " I don't know if I have ever told you that. You make me proud."

I reach out and grab him, hugging him with all I got. "Miles, man. You just don't know. I just—I just wanna thank you. For everything. I love you, man."

"Love you, too, son."

I step back from both of them and exhale again. "Man, it's gonna be hard leaving you guys."

"Don't worry about it. You'll be back in less than two months for my wedding, right?" Miles asks."I wouldn't miss it for the world. By the way, tell Melody I said hello."

"Sure will."

I turn to walk away. Before I go through the security checkpoint, I wave back at them. Sherita stands on her tips and waves over the heads of people passing by. Miles smiles and nods his head to me. I wave back at them, feeling a little tug of sadness in my heart.

There was a time when I couldn't have told you what the future held for me, but as I step forward today, I smile knowing that whatever it is, everything will be a'ight.

ACKNOWLEDGMENTS

I would like to thank my family and friends for encouraging me with this novel. In particular, I would like to thank my wife for never giving up on this book, my parents for supporting my dream of completing it, and Marie Brown for sharing her wisdom as I developed it.

I would also like to thank those of you who consider yourselves fans of my work. It means a lot to me that you have taken the time to journey through my imagination with me.

This novel is nearly ten years in the making, so truly I hope that it finally pays off for all of us.

Ran Walker earned his Bachelor of Arts in English from Morehouse College and holds a Master of Science in Publishing from Pace University and a Juris Doctor degree from George Washington University Law School. He has worked for several magazines, including *The New Yorker*, *American Heritage*, *American Legacy*, *Vibe*, and *Spin*. After leaving publishing, he returned to his home state of Mississippi and practiced law, before yielding to his true calling of writing. He is currently an Assistant Professor of English and Creative Writing at Hampton University.

He is the winner of the 2019 National Indie Author of the Year Award (selected by judges from *Library Journal*, *Publisher's Weekly*, IngramSpark, St. Martin's Press, and *Writer's Digest*), the 2019 Black Caucus of the American Library Association Best Fiction Ebook Award, and the 2018 Virginia Indie Author Project Award for Adult Fiction. He is also the recipient of both a 2005 Mississippi Arts Commission/NEA artist grant and a 2006 artist mini-grant. He served as an Artist-in-Residence with the Mississippi Arts Commission in 2006. Additionally, he is a past participant in the Hurston-Wright Writers Week Workshop and is the recipient of a fellowship from the Callaloo Writers Workshop.

He is the author of seventeen books. His short stories and poetry have appeared in a variety of anthologies.

He lives in Virginia with his wife and daughter.